Looking Back, Moving Forward

Fiction ♦ Poetry ♦ Essays

Edited by

JULIE C ROBINSON

MAWEN ℥ I
HOUSE

We acknowledge the support of the Canada Council for the Arts for our publishing program. We also acknowledge support from the Government of Ontario through the Ontario Arts Council.

Borderlines Writers Circle has been financially supported by the following:

EDMONTON ARTS COUNCIL, EDMONTON COMMUNITY FOUNDATION, ALBERTA ASSOCIATION FOR MULTICULTURAL EDUCATION, WRITERS' GUILD OF ALBERTA

Cover design by Sabrina Pignataro

Library and Archives Canada Cataloguing in Publication

Looking back, moving forward (2018)
    Looking back, moving forward : fiction, poetry, essays / edited by Julie C Robinson.

Issued in print and electronic formats.
ISBN 978-1-988449-52-4 (softcover).--ISBN 978-1-988449-53-1 (HTML).--ISBN 978-1-988449-67-8 (PDF)

    1. Immigrants--Canada--Literary collections. 2. Immigrants' writings, Canadian (English). 3. Canadian literature (English)--21st century.
I. Robinson, Julie C., 1971-, editor II. Title.

PS8237.I45L66 2018   C810.8'03526912   C2018-905274-0
                                                      C2018-905275-9

Printed and bound in Canada by Coach House Printing.

Mawenzi House Publishers Ltd.
39 Woburn Avenue (B)
Toronto, Ontario M5M 1K5
Canada

www.mawenzihouse.com

Dear Jane,
Here's to our years of friendship!
love! LUCIANA.

Literature is the memory of humanity.

ISAAC BASHEVIS SINGER

Contents

Introduction

Jhumpa Lahiri noted that writers have always used their experience of travel, of facing the unknown, of transition from one home to another as material for poems and stories,[1] and this tradition continues in the writers represented here, though this is not the theme evoked by all of them. This anthology offers a taste of the work of members of the Borderlines Writers Circle, a program of the Writers' Guild of Alberta,[2] intended to remove barriers immigrant and multilingual writers may face in their desire to become part of the local writing community or the Canadian literary scene in general. Some pieces are translations into English. Others are hybrid in their approach, presenting two languages in a single work. Some writers have adopted English as their writing language. The pieces here are grouped according to genre—fiction, drama, poetry, journalism, and memoir or personal essay—to enable the reader to easily turn to their favourite, and in the hopes that their curiosity will pull them into the other genres. Some of the authors have provided a short reflection on their work or their writing process.[3] I find these comments invaluable

[1]   Nilanjana Sudeshna "Jhumpa" Lahiri, author of *Interpreter of Maladies* and *The Namesake* in *The New York Times Sunday Book Review*, September 5, 2013
[2]   Borderlines Writers Circle grew out of the Edmonton Writer-in-Exile program. A more complete history can be found at writersguild.ca.
[3]   This approach is modeled after *The Art of the Short Story: 52 Great Authors, Their Best Short Fiction, and Their Insights on Writing*. It is a book I return to again and again.

to the aspiring writer and to the established writer who may find a new kinship with an author here.

Recently, I had the pleasure of co-hosting a forum called "Bridging Cultures Through Writing,"[4] in which writers spoke about what the act of writing meant to them. I came away with a full page of insights: writing enables one to reflect, to understand one's experiences, to understand oneself. Writing brings sensitive issues to the surface and can enable change within a community. Writing—across genres—entertains and educates. And, writing our human stories preserves diversity, preventing a single hegemonic narrative.

The volume you hold in your hands urges the reader to also reflect, experience pleasure, move to a deeper understanding. Some of the stories are an invitation to step into Syria, Somalia, China, Germany—to list a few settings. But only with one foot. The other foot remains in Canada. Each of these authors has been impacted by the experience of relocating, of making home away from home. Each of them has had to reconcile dual identities, with varying degrees of satisfaction. The inescapable position now is one of looking back. The inescapable position of *now* is shaped by one's past. Thus, the title *Looking Back, Moving Forward*.

To say something about what this collection teaches me, or how it makes me feel as a reader, let me begin with reference to Italo Calvino. In a wonderful lecture on the quality of lightness in literature, he suggests that lightness is a reaction to the weight of living. He identifies three forms of lightness: "a lightening of language" or "a verbal fabric that seems weightless"; a description of a psychological process; and, thirdly, visual images of lightness, for example, birds or any kind of flight, or the moon suspended over the earth.[5] In this anthology, lightness is surely at play, and it has nothing to do with denying the realities of this world, but instead helps to come to terms

4   Bridging Cultures Through Writing—Multicultural Writing Forum Series, hosted by Edmonton Chinese Writing Club and Writers' Guild of Alberta, April 15, 2018.

5   Italo Clavino, *Six Memos for the Next Millennium*, translated by Geoffry Brock (Boston: Mariner Books, 2016) 19.

with our fragile and perishable humanity, the real precariousness of our existence.

Susana Chalut's poems illustrate the idea of a weightless verbal fabric: they are reflective and rhythmic. And lightness is there in the images, too—she has given us "the song of the lark" and connected wide open sky with vulnerability. Alma Mancilla's short story "Little Blue Angels" (already in the title we have the weightlessness of angels) is an extraordinary example of reaching after lightness even as the heaviness of reality overtakes her protagonist. Here, Alma deftly offers the reader a psychological experience, the only outcome of which must be compassion. I could cite several more examples of lightness that is inextricably linked to human vulnerability in the works collected here—love, for example, that ecstatic, devastating, abstract and yet so tangible thing, in "Chest Pain," "Blinded by Love," and "Extinct"—but you can read them for yourself.

What makes me sit up and say to my neighbour, "Hey, read this!" is pleasure in the quality of writing, such as, memories rendered in fresh, unexpected, musical language. For example, Luciana Erregue-Sacchi writes, "Alongside the crisscrossing patterns of our discontent / Dye me in the blue hue of your regrets." And "Branched— / we depart, we contort, / we distort our history." Or I am emotionally and intellectually moved, as in Leilei Chen's intimate essay "Life Begins at Forty." True to the genre of the personal essay, Leilei investigates her past choices, rigorously seeks honesty and in so doing creates, even as she discovers, her *self*.[6] While I don't share the details of Leilei's personal history, she mirrors for me, the reader, a way of approaching my own personality, choices, and familial and geographic circumstances in order to understand their meaning. The particulars of her story successfully invoke universal experience.

An equal, if not greater, vulnerability (again this word—so linked to lived experience, to truth) exits in "Running in Munich" where I am transported into past pain and confusion, where events that

---

6 See Phillip Lopate's introduction to *The Art of the Personal Essay* (New York: Anchor Books, 1995).

should never transpire, do. In Mila Philipzig's piece, the essay form is compelled to give way to poetry. This reminds me that literature is an art in which form and content harmonize. We are in the province of the Aesthetic. Its borders are freely open, no passports or visas required.

I once read an article about melancholy as a complex, mature, aesthetic emotion.[7] It stated that the difference between depression and melancholy lies in the quality of reflection which includes pleasure in remembering what was, an appreciation of the value of what has been lost, and the ability to render loss as an aesthetic experience. Melancholy does not exclude grief or sadness but invites something closer to awe and reverence than despair, which may later transform into gratitude. Melancholy is what I feel after reading Aksam Alyousef's play "Hagar," set in war-time Aleppo. I have to sit quietly for a while after the curtain closes.

Each piece in this anthology is a mini-journey in which I can't anticipate at the start where I will end up. I hope that in journeying with these stories you are enriched and encouraged to remember, to process, to build bridges between the transitions in your own life, and to cultivate community. We look back and move forward together. As Clarice Lispector said: "I am a little scared: scared of surrendering completely because the next instant is the unknown. The next instant, do I make it? Or does it make itself? We make it together with our breath." I am honoured to have worked with these writers who have adopted Canada as their home.

Enjoy!

—Julie C Robinson, Edmonton, April 2018

---

7   Emily Brady and Arto Haapla, "Melancholy as an Aesthetic Emotion," *Journal of Contemporary Aesthetics* V. 1, 2003, from http://www.contempaesthetics.org/newvolume/pages/journal.php

fiction.

ALMA MANCILLA

⟋

Little Blue Angels

Lucas's pale gaze wandered along the wall, at the same height where a solitary painting was hanging. His pupils—green, with touches of grey—contracted and distended with the flow of the light, going from right to left, then from left to right, attentive to the slightest sign of movement of something that he—and only he—could see. Ada, as usual, did not move. She knew well that when this happened it was better, safer, to stay still. The spirits had very bad manners; they could get upset or upset Lucas. She wistfully studied the paleness of the painting on the wall, the lively colours of the frame—a reproduction of Klimt's *Kiss* that she had bought years ago, before marrying, when she had wanted to be an artist. The iridescence of the painting's golden frame was blinding and made the room appear unreal.

On the cheap reflecting glass over the painting, at the height of the woman's closed eyes, two lights were shining. Ada knew they came from outside, from the street. They could not be what Lucas was looking at; they were too banal, too earthly. Those lights would not have caught the attention of a child like him. Lucas's pupils were fixed, enlarged, like those of a frightened cat, and his breathing had switched from soft and regular to agitated and fast. These were details, of course. Anyone else would have found them insignificant. Any other person wouldn't have noticed. But not Ada. Ada could feel it, she could *know* the difference.

A few minutes, long and tense, passed before Lucas's breathing came back to normal, his pupils contracted, and colour reappeared on his face.

—Did you see them, Mom?

Ada didn't say a thing. What could she say? She knew that the question was rhetorical, he was not expecting an answer. She wasn't wrong, because as soon as she rose from the sofa where she had been sitting she saw him run down the corridor and disappear into the darkness behind the last door, probably looking for another kind of distraction there in his room. Ada thought it was better this way: that it finished quickly, that Lucas seemed neither to realize nor to remember what had happened. A few minutes later, the familiar buzz of a battery train came out of his room. Ada, in the meantime, had slowly come into the kitchen, stunned—how could it not be so?—and opened the shelf above her head. She set the cereal boxes and the half empty bags aside until she found what she was looking for. The bottle of brandy felt heavy in her hand, as if it were made of lead. It was almost empty, though, because Ada would always need a drink after one of those scenes: a glass, two, sometimes three. The events were worth it. Now, almost six months later, Ada still shivered.

The apparitions had begun on a gray winter day, just after the family had moved to this house. It had happened in the room at the bottom, which now belonged to Lucas. She called them that, the apparitions, as if she knew them firsthand and in spite of the fact that no one, except Lucas, of course, could actually *see* them. Ada had heard that some people would end up getting used to the invisible presences, but not her. Even if she were capable of keeping her composure, whenever her son came into what she called his "trances" she felt as if she was falling into a very deep hole, and it was just because her duties as a mother forced her to be attentive that she hadn't allowed herself, not even once, to close her eyes.

Ada had finished her first glass as she came out again into the living room. She looked around. They were gone, she was sure. She could feel it. Besides, the apparitions always came in waves, and this was the third one this week. Today, they might not see them again. Lucas used to call them "los pequeños angelitos," the tiny little angels. That's what they were, no doubt: little innocent spirits that he would draw on paper sheets, which Ada would later gather up. On the paper they looked like graceful dragonflies, little light-coloured birds flying in a clear sky.

—Moooom! The train has run out of batteries!

—Hold on, Lucas. I'll find you some in a second . . .

Ada poured more brandy and the first sip made her feel better. When she was a child she had had a relative, a godmother, who was a medium. Ada had seen her only once in action, so to speak. Her face was all red, as if she had a fever, she was covered with sweat and her voice sounded hoarse, as if she had a terrible cold. It also seemed that she had fallen asleep, with her eyes wide open. In any case, she seemed to be absent, very far from the dimly lit room full of chairs and shadows, whose windows her mother used to cover with dark curtains every time one of those spirit séances was held. Sometimes, white candles were lighted. Her mother insisted on the colour, lest a dark spirit was summoned instead.

Ada couldn't help a shiver, and she shook her head to clear her mind. It must have been her mother who had passed on to her that strong credulity. Everything had a limit, of course. Her mother used to say that the eyes of her godmother would turn white, like two boiled eggs. About that, Ada had her doubts. Lucas's situation was different. She believed in it a hundred percent. In the books that Ada had borrowed from the library, she had read that the voices of those who saw apparitions changed, and that sometimes the colour of their eyes would turn into the colour of margarine; them expelled foam from the mouth, as though suffering from rabies. Ada was relieved, almost thankful, that none of these things had happened to her Lucas; that his visions were peaceful, quiet, like a river and not like a rough sea.

When Marcos came home, Ada was tempted to tell him what had happened, but she didn't. Marcos didn't like these stories, she knew

that well. They ate their dinner in silence, under the faint light of
the overhead lamp. In his room, Lucas was silent as well, as almost
always when Marcos was at home. But Ada could feel him moving,
coming and going as a caged dog. Then, that night—as every night
when these incidents took place—Ada could not sleep at all. She felt
a strange sense of unease, the entire house was so silent, felt heavy
around her, sunken in a wet and warm somnolence.

—There's a noise in the corridor, said Ada without moving,
buried deep under her blanket.

—No, darling, I have looked twice. You're having these ideas
again . . .

She knew he would not get up, and she tossed around in the
bed, as in a fever. Not altogether asleep, not altogether awake, she
changed her position, she adjusted the pillow. But yes, of course,
there was something. A tapping, some voices. She finally got up on
her tiptoes, trying not to wake up Marcos, who would get up very
early in the morning, and went out into the corridor. She found it
sunken in darkness, except for a few splatters of light here and there
on the wall. She opened the door of the room downstairs to check
on her son. He was sleeping peacefully. Ada didn't approach, but she
could perfectly imagine the warm halo of his breath, the soft wetness
of the sweat on his face. Maybe Marcos was right. There was nothing after all. Or, Lucas would have woken up, he would have been
agitated. Ada came back to bed, where she stayed awake, attentive
to the possibilities. Because if there was anything she was convinced
of, it was that everything happening to Lucas was perfectly *possible*.
She would almost have said *normal*. The apparitions were real, and as
everything real, sooner or later they had to become manifest.

It had all started with small blanks, apparently insignificant moments
of distraction during which Lucas appeared quiet, not moving at
all, as in those cartoons where the image freezes in space. Then, he
would suddenly abandon his toys and run to hide in the closet. At
first, Ada was not worried. After all, that's what kids were like. She

didn't care much either that Lucas wandered in the apartment whispering things, mumbling as if speaking to himself. She had been a little bit like that herself, and Lucas was at an age for it. Actually, she hadn't even seriously thought about the issue until the day Lucas told her he was seeing things.

—What things?

—Things, Mom. People.

Ada had carefully inspected the corridors, every corner of the apartment, the bottom of the trunks, without finding anything strange or abnormal. Then she started asking the neighbors about disappearances, murders, and ghosts. She would have invited her godmother, had she been alive, in order to solve the mystery. Because neither the lack of evidence, nor the fact that no one had ever seen or heard anything could change her mind that what was happening was something supernatural. Ada had just concluded that Lucas was more perceptive, more sensitive than other people. After all, that was not surprising either. It must have come from family. For that reason, when Marcos—a most worldly man—suggested seeing a doctor, Ada was as surprised as she was outraged.

—What do you mean? What doctor can I take him to?

—Ada, listen to yourself. It is obvious something is not all right . . .

—Something is not all right with the house, she objected, as she carefully hung on the wall next to the kitchen the Chinese amulet she had bought that same morning. The saleslady had assured her it was a powerful tool, useful against all sorts of spirits, including poltergeists.

—Oh, Ada, you wouldn't believe, even for a second . . .

But Ada wouldn't listen, and Marcos had left, upset as usual when Ada wouldn't listen. He knew her nature, her stubbornness, her manias too well to stay and argue with her. Ada knew that because he loved her (she was much younger, much more creative, much more everything that Marcos was not), he would swallow his anger and wait until later, for her better humour to return in order to solve the argument. However, a few minutes later she heard him talking on the phone, in the corridor. He sounded worried.

—Yes, yes. If she didn't drink so much. If, at least, she had kept her job . . . Helena, I don't know what to do anymore . . .

Ada decided to ignore him. Not that she didn't care, but she had already enough problems with the apparitions. Wasn't he, besides, the one who had advised her to take a break? Hadn't he told her that some rest would be good for her? Hadn't he insisted, finally convincing her, to stay at home, to write from here and not in the newspaper office where she had had a job? Ada glanced at the mess on her desk, covered with papers she hadn't even looked at in months. She immediately tried to justify herself; with what was going on with Lucas, such a mess was not surprising. To think that everything could be happening inside Lucas's head—wasn't this what Marcos tried to imply?—seemed just crazy. No matter how hard she tried, she just couldn't figure out from where, how, why something like that could happen to Lucas. And what did Marcos know, anyway? He, the one who did not believe in anything? She had never seen the little angels herself—not with her own eyes—but she *knew* they were there. She could feel them. Of course, she could feel them! Tiny motionless presences, floating in the room. She could *almost* see them.

"You want to believe you feel them, Ada," Marcos would rebuke her whenever she used that argument. No, of course not. How could it all be fake, the chill on her back, the gooseflesh when she entered a dark room? Marcos was always seeing problems, foretelling diseases. Once, he had taken her to an oncologist because of a small pain in one breast. Marcos was a bird of ill omen. He was the one seeing things that weren't there. Why couldn't he simply accept what was obvious? That there are things some people can see and some others cannot? But no, not Marcos . . . It was as if he wasn't ready. As if he could not accept that among all people he was a chosen one, fortunate to be close to someone with such a special gift.

Ada looked at the clock. It was almost two. She hurriedly drank a sip of brandy directly from the bottle while she waited, sitting in front of the tiny table of her kitchen, for her sister-in-law to come back. She had shown up without warning and had asked to use the washroom. She came back quickly and silently, and Ada was startled when she saw her there, right behind her.

—You really scared me, Helena! said Ada as she tried to hide the bottle behind the market bags her sister-in-law had brought for her.

Helena tried to smile—something she didn't do easily—and she sat at the table. Ada reluctantly offered her another cup of coffee. She didn't like these unannounced visits, even if they were under the excuse of bringing her something or, as everyone said, helping her. In her experience, nothing good could come out of these visits. She was glad when her sister-in-law said she couldn't stay longer because she had an appointment at three. They talked a few minutes about everything and nothing—they did not usually have much to talk about—while the light entered through the kitchen window, throwing violet reflections on the angled face of Helena.

—Are you all right, Ada?—she said finally, in a tone that Ada didn't like at all. Helena's eye wandered from the numerous crosses on the door frame to the many images of the virgin, and from there to the horseshoe hanging from the ceiling. Ada caught Helena's grimace, her look of open disapproval when she noticed the Chinese amulets, and the pots full of water that literally covered the corridor.

—Marcos is worried, Ada. I hope you know what I mean . . .

So Marcos had gone to gossip to her about Lucas. Ada shrunk on her chair, offended.

—Ada, why don't you talk to someone about it?

Ada felt the room was turning around. It seemed to her that the virgin and the saints on the wall were staring at her with inquisitive eyes. For a second, she wanted the apparitions to show themselves, now, while her sister-in-law was still there. But Helena wouldn't know how to keep this to herself. She would be telling it around to everybody. It was better this way. Ada calmed down, trying to convince herself that, as usual, the apparitions would wait until she and

Lucas were alone.

—Whatever, I have to go. Ada, if you need anything, anything at all, just give me a call. Did you hear me? Jesus, Ada, it's not good for you to be alone at home for long hours. Look at you, for Christ's sake! So young, and dressed as if you were attending a funeral!

Ada felt sorry about that woman, so vain, so made up, so ignorant of so many things. What could she know about her life, her concerns? She didn't even have children. Helena grabbed her coat from the back of the chair, and it seemed the encounter was at last coming to an end, when she stopped at the doorstep.

—You are fooling yourself, Ada, she said.

At that moment Ada hated her. Helena had never been interested in them, in their marriage. Ada knew she was jealous of her luck—in spite of being so attractive, Helena was, at her age, still alone. She was jealous that Ada had Lucas. How happy she would be, that harsh woman, to know that Lucas had a problem! Ada felt a wave of warmth on her face and she knew the apparitions were approaching. There was nothing to do. Helena was already out in the corridor when Lucas came out of his room, walking slowly towards the door with a bear under his arm. Ada wanted to close the door right away, but Helena stopped her.

—It's better to accept the problem, Ada. I can recommend a doctor.

—All right, all right. I'll go if that makes you both feel better, said Ada without thinking. She really wanted to close that door, fearful that the spirits could run away. Or worse, fearful that something even more terrible, more ominous, could enter the house. As if, in her carelessness, she was about to let their surroundings be besieged, invaded by the additional darkness of another presence.

In spite of Ada's protests, Marcos and Helena arranged for the appointment that same week. What was the rush? And then, at such an inconvenient hour, because of Lucas's school. Ada had tried to change the date, or to schedule for the afternoon. Finally, Marcos insisted in driving them himself. The whole way Lucas had sat silently at the back, crouched on the seat, no doubt intimidated by the change in his routine. Ada wouldn't stop talking to him, trying to make him smile a bit and ignoring the reproachful glances that Marcos threw at her every time. In the clinic, the doctor asked Marcos to wait outside. The doctor's office was light purple and had a faint scent of perfume. Ada had decided on the spot that she felt all right in there, but the doctor appeared to her distant and insensitive. It bothered her that he wouldn't stop asking banal, useless questions: how was she feeling? Was she eating properly? Then, noticing her impatience, he suddenly became silent and looked at her for a few seconds before starting again.

—Let's talk a bit about your son, Ada. Lucas.

She was startled. She didn't like the way he pronounced the name of her son. She regretted having come here, brought Lucas. All this was wrong. This would do nothing but scare him. Ada wanted to say something, but she felt overwhelmed by the office, by its purple walls, by the doctor's glasses. She was feeling warm, and wanted the appointment to finish quickly, to finish right away.

—Ada, please don't stand up so soon, the doctor said when he saw her looking for her purse. —I am saying this because I think we can find a solution together . . .

A solution? What solution? Now she understood, at last! She had the clear certainty that Marcos knew it as well. Helena knew it. These doctors, they were all the same. If they thought Lucas was not right in the head, that she would accept . . . No, they were wrong. She would never consent to something like that. She would not put Lucas in an institution, like those places they showed in the movies. Just the idea of spending all this money on a psychiatrist for nothing but listening to herself talk about her own life seemed repulsive. She felt Lucas growing impatient at her side, and she thought he would burst out crying. She looked at him, nestling in the folds of the sofa, his head on the soft headrest, his golden curls scattered on the leather as shiny as a piece of obsidian. For no particular reason, she wanted to cry.

—I . . . , she babbled, feeling her voice breaking, refusing to obey her. She was surprised by the fragile sound of her own voice. By her own screams. By the strength that made her resist all the attempts of the doctor to calm her. She felt dizzy, nauseated. She saw Marcos hastily entering the room and she felt many arms trapping her. Then, everything went dark.

When she woke up she was lying on the sofa, at home. Marcos was there, talking on the phone.

—Yes, she is waking up. I'll call you back.

—Where is Lucas? she asked, still feeling anxious and confused.

—Shhh, he said. —Everything will be fine. The doctor gave you a sedative.

Ada wanted to get up but she couldn't. Over her head she could see floating clouds. Clouds, or some kind of fog. Was she sleeping? In dreams, she had heard words like severe depression, traumatic shock, schizophrenia. When she opened her eyes again, she saw them. It was the first time, and it was indeed astonishing: they were there, in the corner, just over her head, and they were exactly like Lucas had described them: blue and bright. Their presence seemed to her so painful and at the same time so overwhelming that tears came to her eyes. Marcos came to check on her from time to time, and he must have noticed her bewilderment, because he sat by her side.

—It's the sedative, Ada. The doctor said it could cause hallucinations.

Ada didn't say anything. Because she could feel Lucas approaching, touching her face and curling next to her. She felt calmed and protected. She could remember the day Lucas was born. The life pouring out of her in warm waves of diluted blood. She wanted time to stop, the universe to be reduced, for once, to that unique moment. She wished that, even if only for a second, it was all that would exist.

Dark gray days followed, one after the other, chained to an autumn that was leaving just too soon. Winter came, fierce as it hadn't been in years. At home, buried under the weight of seclusion, the apparitions grew in number. At least that's what Ada thought, her days spent seeing Lucas running about, turning off the lights, turning on the electronic equipment, constantly throwing his toy trains around. Ada looked for comfort in the virgins on the wall, and they spread out their veils of tenderness. There was no way of convincing her to return to the doctor's office, but to her it was evident something must be done. Marcos decided to play along with her. He helped her to fill the rooms with amulets of all kinds, he burned incense, and he even went out one morning to buy the votive candles to Saint Michael that she had so much wanted. They called someone to clean the house. The corridors were saturated with prayers, a strong tickling smell of bay and garlic rising from the small brazier they had bought for the occasion. But the apparitions refused to leave.

Ada knew there was but one thing to do: to leave that home. Wasn't it here that it had all begun? Wasn't it between these walls that their once peaceful life had turned into this? Ada started to look at the walls in a different way, estranged from the corners, the nooks, the corridors. She had never liked that apartment anyway. It was so small, so unsuitable for a child. She wanted a house. A house like the one she had lived in when she was a young girl. A luminous house, full of sun, and not this dark horrid place Marcos had taken them to. No wonder the spirits had been disturbed! When she was a child there used to be flowers in the corridors. Real flowers, not the fake plastic butterflies they had in the building, good only to collect dust and mites. To her, it was decided.

One night during dinner she dared to announce it.

—We have to move out Marcos, she said, trying to make it sound obvious and natural.

To her surprise, he didn't say no. He didn't say anything, actually. He just looked at her from behind the coagulated green of his eyes, a glance that was at the same time tired and infinitely sad. For a few days she kept herself so busy that she barely felt Lucas's presence, and even the apparitions must have had the feeling of being left behind, because they remained silent, hostile, cruel towards those who were leaving.

The new house was bright and full of light. From the huge window of the living room you could see all the faces of the sun and the changing phases of the moon. There was a fountain in the garden with two angels with tiny wings and mischievous looks. Marcos had found it, just as she wanted it. A new life was about to start. Ada breathed with relief, sure that, at last, they had left behind that short interlude of shadow in what should have been, she thought, a journey of light. She felt appeased knowing that here, in this place, nothing could happen to Lucas. That he, too, was finally safe.

Several weeks of quiet domestic confusion went slowly by. Even Marcos had a smile on his face, seeing her like this, coming and going as she unpacked. The afternoon when she finished setting the last piece of furniture in its place, and after the last of the boxes was empty, she was exhausted. Placing Lucas's things had been a specially demanding task. Ada sat there, in their new luminous living room where the sun would soon set. Suddenly, as if she were coming out of a dream, she shivered. Lucas. She hadn't seen him the whole day. She couldn't tell, actually, when she had seen him last.

She panicked. She went running down the luminous corridors, and was relieved when she found him in the living room, sitting on the sofa from where she had just got up.

—Come here, Lucas, she said. —I'll get your jersey. It's better for you to wear it.

Ada was approaching Lucas when Marcos stood in her way. In the afternoon light her husband's face seemed suddenly full of compassion and, at the same time, exceedingly old.

—Ada, he started, frowning, his eyes surrounded by deep wrinkles and full with tears. —When will you accept that Lucas is dead? It's been more than two years. You have tried everything, Ada. Lucas is gone.

Ada looked again towards the sofa. Sitting there, Lucas's gaze was soft as looked at something far away. A thread of drool dropped on his little hands, flowed onto his lap. His face had the shocked face of a sculpture, and on his motionless legs she saw, all in blue, the last drawing he had made. From a distance they looked like flies. Dragonflies. The little blue angels.

Ada felt confused. Then Lucas looked up and smiled at her with infinite tenderness and waved goodbye with his hand. Afternoon light descended upon the house, shining brightly, flashing a glittering orange into which Lucas finally vanished. Ada stared at her own gaunt and aged reflection, right there at the bottom of a mirror she had recently hung on the wall. Her bloodshot eyes, her face on which shone, like two firebrands, the black rings of her silent loss. She saw herself in the hospital, at the bedside where that life, so short, had extinguished. "A cerebral infarction. Extremely rare at that age, but irreversible. Deadly." Ada wanted to scream, just as she had wanted to at that time. To howl. But now, as then, she couldn't.

Marcos didn't say anything. He held his wife, and at that moment Lucas's jersey fell on the floor. Using her last strength Ada knelt to pick it up. She stayed down, sat there in the dark with her son's jersey in her arms, thinking about all the things she had brought with her, all those useless toys, all the clothes no one would ever wear again. Then, at last, she cried. She was not afraid, not anymore. She couldn't feel anything. She knew life was a blink of light. Or, more likely, life was a window in an endless and unfathomable darkness.

The reddish light that announced the arrival of evening finally flooded the room, swallowing Ada and Marcos into it; it was warm and beautiful, a light that, nevertheless, did not offer any consolation.

Ada thought again about her dead child, about how long, how unbearable was the road that was opening ahead of her.

—Don't worry, Ada. We will solve it, said Marcos, whose presence Ada had almost forgotten about.

He was lying, of course. Marcos was lying. There are things that are irreparable. That nothing and no one can bring back. Ada shivered. Hadn't Lucas been there that same morning? Hadn't he been there all those days? Had she been dreaming? Inside her head thoughts flowed like in a torrent, furious, rapid, uncontrollable. Was she truly losing her mind? What if she kept seeing him? Then, suddenly, she felt terrified to think about the other possibility: what if she really *did not* see him, ever again? Her mind switched for a second between the two possibilities, unable to decide which one was worse. If she had to choose between seeing her son once more—even for a second, even in an illusion—and her sanity, what would she pick? It did not matter anymore. What had to be, would be. Ada closed her eyes as the light around her receded, until the day faded, like the flame of an extinguishing candle.

Author's Note

It is well known that to translate means to betray: *Traduttore, traditore*, or so they say. This might be true or false, depending on who translates and what is translated. Probably poetry is harder to translate than prose, given its inwardness, but there's also prose that is particularly difficult, if not altogether impossible to translate. I don't even know if one has the *right* to translate one's own work. It does take courage, for sure. The more I think about it, the more I'm convinced it should not be done except in case of great need, but what this great need might be, I'm uncertain. I have asked a couple of writer friends if they would like to try it, and they all said no. Why would someone want to *translate* when it is possible to *write*, especially when time for writing is usually so scarce? In short: let others do that work.

Trying to write in a language that is not your first (whether from scratch or in translation) is something of a masochistic task, one that seeks accomplishment amidst the constant reminder of one's limitations. And still, here we are, writers landed in foreign lands, presumably with nothing better to do than translating what we've written in another language. I feel a hint of discomfort when I think about this; also, Nabokov, Canetti, Becket, Conrad come to mind, all those who chose or were forced to write in a language different from their mother tongue and succeeded. Pessoa once wrote that the

Portuguese language was his homeland, and then one remembers that his first works were written in English. His phrase, beautiful as it is, brings to mind the idea of a unique place with which we identify totally and fully, defined by the boundaries of language. Where is this "homeland" located, especially in times like ours? Does it correspond to an actual geographic space? With a community? Or, as I suspect, can it be that it is nowhere and everywhere at the same time, a homeland that takes root in literary traditions and what they represent?

Borges, at times, was close to translating himself. He was comfortable enough in English (which he learned at the same time as Spanish) and he collaborated very closely with one of his translators. Strangely, I've read that these translations are considered among the worst available of his work in English. This is partly because of the immense freedom that Borges allowed himself when trying to pour his own fiction into the container of a new language. In one of his bright essays Coetzee mentions that Borges didn't like, in particular, the use of words that he thought too "violent" for English: *pérfido*, *perverso*, *abominable*, that were all, at his request, softened in the English versions. The justification by Borges himself was that Spanish and English have "two quite different ways of looking at the world." For sure, one of the things I've learned when trying to translate my work is that the narrative voice expressed in Spanish must struggle at times to find its way in English. I'm also perfectly conscious that this might be, in my case, an effect of me not being a native English speaker and not a danger of translation itself. I also realize how much one is tempted to "improve" or alter what was imperfectly written in the original.

Translating *Pequeños angelitos azules*, as my piece here was originally entitled, was definitely an enriching experience, one that allowed me some unusual insights into the mechanisms of language in general, and into the way I have built and keep building my own fiction. To what extent I have betrayed myself, I can't tell. I hope this betrayal has not been as noticeable as to make this story less authentic. I also hope that the reader will find that it was worth the experience. Any writer, any translator, could not ask for more.

—

"Little Blue Angels" is from *The Slime of the Snail and Other Stories*, IMC, México, 2014 (author's translation).

ANAMOL MANI

Chest Pain

Sunday

I pulled the curtain and opened the window. A soothing breeze gusted in to touch all four corners of my room. A few papers on the table blew off to the floor.

The sky was a deep blue, unfathomably spread out above me. The radiant sun added to its color. My eyes were dazzled by the brightness. I blinked and shook my head. With both hands, I combed my disheveled hair and braced myself up. A flock of birds flew past my window and away. If people could fly like the birds, where would we reach?

As the breeze caressed my face, I closed my eyes. When I opened them again, I could see the city scattered with upthrust buildings. Vehicles passed in front of my house. The leaves rustled on the trees outside on the road. A sweet sound.

Today, an unusual patient was admitted to the hospital. I was busy the entire day looking after him. He said his chest was hot, that it burned. He felt pain in his chest.

We ran the usual tests. There were no anomalies in the results of blood and urine. The preliminary report didn't show any problems in his chest. His blood pressure was normal.

I prescribed Ibuprofen to reduce the pain in his chest.

Monday

There weren't many patients in my department today. I went to see the patient. His eyes had reddened and his eyelashes were sticky. His face was unnaturally dark, lips chapped. "Didn't you sleep the whole night?"

"No, I could not sleep, doctor."

"Why?"

"Unlike during the day, my chest did not burn and there was no pain. But I could not sleep."

"Your eyes clearly say that you did not sleep."

He kept quiet. My eyes were fixed on him. Still, he didn't look any more serious today. I suggested that he discharge himself and go back home. But he wouldn't listen.

Instead, he kept rubbing his chest with his hand and said, "Doctor, I want to stay with you, in the hospital."

"Why? There's nothing wrong with you. You don't need to stay here."

"Doctor, all I feel is pain ripping through my chest. Every tear is a shredding pain. It burns. Please. I feel secure here. Please don't discharge me now."

I stared into his eyes, as they filled with tears. His face grew pale. His forehead was squeezed into a thin fold of skin. He took hold of my gown.

"Doctor, this is nothing but a wound made of tears. Please believe me. It burns me from inside, from very deep inside. Kill me, please."

I have treated a lot of patients, but I had never seen anyone like him in my years of practice. I said, "The hospital is not to die, it is to live. We are here to appeal for life, not for anyone's death." I again ordered for his total pathological work-up. I took off his upper dress to examine his chest. Even with my stethoscope, everything seemed perfectly fine. There were no signs of internal injury. But any injury that burned him from the inside couldn't be detected with a stethoscope.

"Doctor, pain caused this wound," he repeated, curling up. In a fragile voice he said, "Doctor, take another look. Inspect my chest deeply. There is a big wound, a big wound. Please, please doctor."

I ordered a CT-scan. I already knew the results of his X-ray. I checked his torso again, looked for signs of internal infection. I found nothing. Everything came out normal. I kept reading the report. I read it twice, but could not find any problem. I wondered if I should refer him to a psychiatrist. I pondered for a while. If there was nothing wrong in the report, he should be safe from anything dangerous. Eventually, I decided to keep him under observation for a few days in case symptoms surfaced.

"Do you smoke?" I asked him.

"No, I don't."

"Drink?"

"No, I don't." He shook his head. "No doctor, I don't do anything."

"Do you normally sleep well?"

"Yes, I sleep 'till late in the morning."

"How is your appetite?"

"My appetite is good. Usually I start my day with a cup of coffee, I eat lunch in the afternoon, and a full dinner at night."

"So, do you work out heavily every morning?"

"No, I am not any sort of athlete. I don't tend to leave my bed until 8:30 in the morning."

The conversation ended. I went out.

Tuesday

Today was his third day in hospital. He was rubbing his back with pain, rubbing his hand on his chest and stomach. He tried to arch up from the bed, and screamed.

"It burns. Oh, it burns. Please, doctor, I cannot take it. Kill me. Or cut some of my veins to take this pain out." He held his chest tightly. Gradually he became quieter. His eyes were pale. I could see tears streaming out from the corners of his eyes.

"What addiction do you have that you have hidden?"

"Why would I tell lies to you? I promise, doctor, I don't drink. I don't smoke."

"What makes you suffer and burn from inside, then?"

"Poisonous tears in my heart, doctor, but you cannot see it."

I kept looking at him without speaking.

Slowly, he raised his head and looked at me and said, "You must be thinking I'm nuts, but believe me, that's not true. This is nothing but pain given by tears, I'm sure of it. I knew from the very beginning that you'd be unable to discover my wound." It seemed as if he was the doctor, not me.

I smiled and said, "Are you the specialist now?"

"There is a big pain in my chest. My chest is ripped open and there are holes, each burning and full of painful blisters. Every second, I can feel those blisters burst."

"How? This is impossible."

"This is the reality, doctor."

"But how?"

He closed his eyes for a while, then opened them, blinking. Rubbing his lips together, he tried to turn towards the right. His face gleamed so that he seemed to smirk. He said, "Unusually *that* evening, she lay her head on my chest, weeping, and she said she wanted to live with me. She asked me to take her with me." He looked at me, as thought trying to read my face. Then, avoiding my look, he furrowed his brow. Heaving a long sigh, he said, "I was unemployed. Do you know the meaning of unemployment in the city? I did not have a proper place to live. I was hardly surviving. I could not muster up the courage to accept her request."

I asked, "When did this happen?"

"It happened three days before her marriage." His face darkened and he pressed his lips together. He looked at the wall behind me.

"And what happened?"

"The same evening, for the first time, I felt a pain deep inside my chest. Now she belongs to someone else. It happens in life. It is better that one should try to forget the past. I know that she still loves me. My cowardice broke our three-year relationship."

He fixed his gaze at the wall while he clenched and unclenched.

"You will be fine soon," I said. "This is all about your psychology."

He closed his eyes.

Wednesday

He mentioned his pain. I gave him medicine to soothe him. He wanted to tell me something. I gave him my time.

"Doctor, she has entered my heart so entirely that I cannot remove her even though I want to," he said. "Even in the open wind, under the star-studded sky, I try to forget, but I imagine her. I observe the moon's shadow, the dew and the dark night, but all I wish is to hold her once more and cry. Thinking about all these things makes me feel that life is uncertain, unclear, and deep like the night." He kept quiet for a while. He turned his head towards me. "Doctor, do you ever remember the one you loved the most? Have you ever loved anyone more than yourself?"

"Hmm."

He pulled his hair with both hands and yawned. "I don't understand why she keeps haunting me. She dwells inside my heart like a scar. Why do I remember her so much, even though she's someone else's now? Why do I stare in the mirror of the past and hurt myself?"

I tried consoling him. "It's not good to make yourself sad remembering the past. You need rest now. Don't think so much, take rest."

"That very past is creating this problem. It does not allow me to take a rest, Doctor."

"Don't think too much."

"I try my best to not think about anything, but as the pain begins, I remember that day when she cried leaning on my chest."

I just stared at him.

He said, "Do tears contain any acid which goes deep down into the chest and causes this burning and pain?"

"No, tears do not contain any acid. They are just a medium to express one's sadness. They do no harm to the body."

Raising a finger, in a commanding voice, he said, "There is certainly something in tears, Doctor. You should never let your beloved lean on your chest and cry, Doctor. Never let your lover cry over your heart."

Friday

The nurses told me that he had been suffering even worse since the morning. I entered his room. He was rubbing his chest in slow circles. His eyes were red and swollen. His hair was uncombed. His body trembled so that not even two nurses could control him. Before I could do anything to normalize his condition, he lay prostrate on the bed, holding his chest, his hands and feet stretched out tautly. He was breathing faster. Making a face, he moved his head and became restless for a while. After some time, he became still.

Examining his heartbeat and pulse, the nurse said, "It seems his heartbeat has stopped, Doctor."

I pulled out my stethoscope to check for myself. His eyes were closed, his lips tight together. Many patients die in front of a doctor. Many patients have died in front of me. His death was different. I could not diagnose his illness. The only complaint he had was the pain in his chest. I felt the heat from inside my body. I could feel the sweat on my forehead. A question lingered in my mind. Was it the tears of his girlfriend that had caused the pain in his chest?

Saturday

This is the day after his death, the seventh since his admission to the hospital. His room empty now. No matter how hard I tried, I couldn't find the cause of his pain. With all this technology at my disposal, I still could not discover his problem. Why did he get better for a time and then fall severely ill the next moment? Everything looked normal in his tests. There are wounds inside every person that science cannot discover. Was his pain truly caused by his lover's tears, like he said? CT-scan, X-ray showed nothing. Was it really the tears? As a doctor, why did I fail to discover his true illness? How does a patient die with no visible wounds? Indeed, there is always room for innovation. But it is the failure of medicine when a patient's disease isn't discovered, when a patient can't be helped. I'm thinking that death challenges science to look at other ways to show those invisible wounds.

Sunday

"How can this happen?"

While I was approaching a new patient's room, I heard a woman talking inside.

"Before dying, he said his chest was wounded by the tears of his beloved," she continued.

"Exactly," a second voice replied. "Really, do the tears of love hurt the chest or the heart?"

I realized that they were nurses.

"It should not have happened," said the first nurse.

"Yes, if the tears of one's beloved can make such a wound, then there would be many in the world who would carry such injuries."

"But people say that uncanny things happen in love."

"Yes, the entire world revolves around love."

"Seems the world exists because of love."

"Did you hear his story? How his beloved lay on his chest, crying, and how that wounded him, deep inside? How he died from wounds inflicted by love?"

"Look at her," said the first nurse. "If there were no love in this world, why would she fall unconscious when she heard the news of his death?"

The second nurse said, "Is it true, do you think? That her tears infected his heart?"

I entered the room at that point.

"Doctor, you're here."

It was the first nurse. She was arranging medicines in a cart, on her way to go to the next room. The other nurse was standing with a pen and a board.

"Look here, Doctor." The nurse gave the board to me before I had even looked at the patient.

"Did that patient, the one who died, did he have any relatives?" I asked her.

"Yes, there is a middle-aged woman."

"And?"

"She fainted when she heard about his death."

"How is she now?"

"Pulse rate is fine, as well as blood pressure. But she is still unconscious."

"Okay." I moved towards the patient. She was covered half way with a green blanket. Many things happened at once—my chest became heavy, sweat broke out on my forehead and my bladder felt full. I lost all strength in my legs and my hands. I felt a sudden pain in my head. My hands were trembling. I turned around slowly and went to stand by the window and closed my eyes.

The nurse asked, "Doctor, are you okay?"

The other nurse said, "Doctor, what happened?"

I slowly turned but could not face them. My body felt heavy, it was difficult to take even a step towards the bed. But I managed to walk towards the patient. The nurses were staring at me, wide-eyed.

"Doctor . . . Do you know who she is?"

I caressed the patient's forehead and combed her hair with my fingers. I said, "She is my wife."

Author's Note

I think every individual in the world, regardless of where they belong, has untold or unwritten stories stacked up in their minds. Those seemingly trivial stories carry a vast reality of life. I want to communicate through my stories daily happenings and the time we are living in. We are living in an era dominated by technology. But technological advancement has led us to a virtual world beyond reality. The time has come for us to start thinking if we are actually heading in the right direction. I ask myself what will happen if the virtual world takes over the real world, threatening the very existence of human beings.

Writing is my passion. Through my characters, I try to view life from a different angle. It is a great opportunity for me to meet and engage in conversation with these characters. I keep thinking about them while running my daily errands.

My stories are included in the curriculum of grade seven in Nepal. The stories are being taught and read the way I wanted them to. Sometimes readers (kids in particular) ask me if the characters are real or if the main character is myself. Those questions always make me happy and make me feel that my work is being praised.

Two students of Tribhuwan University in Nepal have done their theses on my stories. In one of them, the student has explored how gender issues are presented, and in the other, the researcher has explored how technology has affected human emotions. Also, five other researchers have done master's theses on me and my style of writing.

MOHAMED ABDI

—

Blinded by Love

Liban's love for Sagal was intense. He went to her house every other night. Sagal's mother knew what he was up to, and so did her father. But Mogadishu wasn't as peaceful as it used to be. Although different Somali clans lived side by side, in their neighbourhood lately things had been deteriorating. Clannish chants were heard all over the place. Some families moved to other neighbourhoods while others left the capital for elsewhere in the country. People accused each other. The Loodin clan was accused of plundering the country's resources, whereas the Leexin clan was alleged to have caused havoc and instability in the capital. There were signs of war. Hooligans in every corner of the city snatched things, hijacked cars, and broke into houses. Armed bandits killed government soldiers inside the capital.

People lived in perpetual fear and frustration. A natural curfew governed the city. People couldn't walk after sunset. They remained in their homes. The capital, especially downtown, lost its beauty and turned into a ghost town.

As security matters in the capital deteriorated, a group of elders comprised of the country's clans sat down and issued a decree. Their aim was to lessen the severe tension between the government and some clans, the Leexin clan being the main one. But these efforts were futile; tension continued. In the evenings, machine gun fire could be heard in the northern parts of the city, as soldiers and armed bandits exchanged fire.

Liban couldn't meet often with Sagal so he told her that he wanted to marry her.

"I'll talk to my parents," she said.

"What if your parents don't agree?" he asked.

"Let's see." But she didn't think about it further. Sagal knew that both her parents weren't comfortable with someone from the Loodin clan. What would happen if they gave their daughter to such a man? Customarily, most Somalis intermarry, including those from the Leexin and Loodin clans. Liban never imagined that one day he would be asked what his clan was. He thought all Somalis were from one ethnicity.

People began vacating their homes, moving in different directions, carrying their belongings in their hands and on their heads. Many families moved from Liban's neighbourhood and moved west.

He asked, "Father, why are these families moving out?"

"They're afraid of possible war and they belong to the Loodin clan, our clan."

"Do we relate to all these families?" Liban asked.

"Yes, we do."

Liban was dumbfounded and realized how bad the situation was. And Sagal was perplexed; she couldn't fathom for what reason people would kill each other. She asked her father, "Is it only because of clan loyalty that people kill each other, or there are other reasons?"

"This president belongs to the Loodin clan, and our clan wants to topple him," he said, looking her in the eye.

"What will happen if our clan overthrows the government?"

"We'll be victorious and rule."

"What would happen to Liban's clan?" she asked.

"That, I couldn't tell," answered her father.

In the following week, the situation in the city got worse, forcing many thousands to flee. Sheik Omar, Liban's father, was among them but Liban remained in Mogadishu, going between his mother's house and Sagal's. His mother warned him, "Don't go to Sagal's house if your father's already left the capital."

"What's the matter, mother?" he asked. "I've no problems with Sagal's family. Besides, I want to marry her."

"My son, they belong to the Leexin clan, and you belong to the Loodin clan. The two clans are enemies. You should know that."

Sheik Omar's house became an abandoned place. Nobody slept in it or used its washroom since he left.

The war intensified between government troops and armed men from the Leexin clan. Even Fadumo Guled, Liban's mother, and her family couldn't remain in the capital. They fled to Tiinley. Liban wanted to go with her, but she rejected the idea. She advised him to go with his father and family. So he hopped on a bus and left Mogadishu and caught up with his father and siblings in Lamadhaafo. Lamadhaafo was five hundred kilometres southwest of Mogadishu. On the bus it was chaos. There were children crying all over the place, and suckling mothers with uncovered breasts attended to their children. Each seat was taken by more than one person. Passengers held to poles and ropes. People had wrapped their foreheads with handkerchiefs. They coughed, complained, and cursed.

Liban thought of Nurto, his stepmother, and her babies. Amran, Nurto's daughter, was five years old, but she had two younger siblings: a boy named Guled, and a girl named Nasra. Guled was three years old; Nasra, one. Sheik Omar had moved his family before things worsened. Food and gas had become scarce and prices had skyrocketed in Mogadishu.

In Lamadhaafo, things were a bit better than they were in the capital. Food was cheaper and available. People who had never been to Lamadhaafo overcrowded its roads.

They occupied different buildings, many of which were owned by the government. They didn't know when they might return to their homes. "Who benefits from this war?" Liban wondered. He and Sagal were far apart now. A relative had given shelter to his family in the town. Two rooms were designated for them, one of which was shared by Sheik Omar and his sons, Liban and Ahmed. It was not adequate shelter, but there was no choice.

Lamadhaafo proved to be unsafe. War advancing from Mogadishu threatened the town. Those who didn't want to get hurt fled again with their families. They headed to Kenya. Liban couldn't stomach the situation. He walked to his father and said, "We can't leave Lamadhaafo. Mogadishu will be okay. Let's wait here for a while." But the safety of the children, women, and elders was crucial.

Sheik Omar's family was one among many weary families from different parts of the capital. JinArag's was one of them. Sheik Omar and JinArag knew each other. JinArag was known to be able to foretell events.

"What would you say of our situation?" Sheik Omar asked him.

JinArag craned his neck, looked around, and said, "Our prospect of getting back to Mogadishu isn't great."

"What does that mean?" Liban asked frantically.

"It's going to be a long war," JinArag said.

Liban brushed off JinArag's statement, saying, "I'll soon get back home."

JinArag and other families headed out to Kenya to seek refuge. A week after JinArag's departure, things worsened in Lamadhaafo. Nothing could be bought. Everything was too expensive, and Liban's prospect of getting back to Mogadishu diminished. Liban and his family eventually headed to Kenya in the back of a truck. They embarked on a perilous road called Lama-mare, a very thin road furnished with thorny trees. People were fearful of the road and its thick, lurking dangers. Parents clung to their children, lest a branch of a tree overhead snatched them away. Women and children wore pale faces, because in Lamadhaafo, they didn't have enough nutrition and they had lived in constant fear. But remaining in Lamadhaafo or getting back to the capital had proved impossible. Along with other families, Sheik Omar's family was on one big truck. More than twenty persons were crammed in. People felt suffocated and continually gasped for air. Sheik Omar covered his face against the scorching sun and said, "I don't understand what they gain from this chaos."

Liban asked, "Are you part of the trouble?"

"No, we're not," his father replied.

"Yes, we're part of the problem because we share lineage with Siyad Barre," said a male passenger. "Anyone that belongs to the Loodin clan is afraid of repercussions, even if they didn't do anything wrong. I don't get it. That is a sick way of thinking."

President Barre was ousted after fierce war and destruction in the capital. Not every Loodin clan member was an accomplice of President Barre, and not every Leexin clan member was an avid enemy of the Loodin clan.

The truck, carrying Liban and his family, eventually arrived in a northeastern part of Kenya and they were put in a temporary refugee camp called Idag. The camp would be later relocated to another part of the northeastern province. Like other families, Sheik Omar's family lined up for plastic tents, food rations, and utensils. They had only brought clothes, a few blankets, and some other portable items. They were penniless refugees. They used to hear about refugees and the challenges they went through. The Sheik and his family didn't know what lay ahead for them.

"Father, do you know if Sagal's family left Mogadishu?" Liban asked.

"I don't know, but many families from the Leexin clan fled the city; they may not have gone far."

"If they fled, where would they go?"

"They would go towards Degta-kale, not that far," the Sheik replied. Liban asked questions as if he wanted the exact whereabouts of Sagal's family.

"I'm going back to see Sagal's family," Liban said to his father.

"What? You're going back into danger!"

"Father, nothing will happen to me."

"Why are you saying 'nothing will happen to me'? The capital has become a dangerous place." Standing in front of his white tent in the scorching heat, Liban put his palm on his forehead and combed his hair backwards. His father walked away angrily.

Nurto came out of the tent and said to Liban, "Everyone is leaving

Mogadishu. Why are you saying 'I'm going back'?"

"But we haven't done anything wrong, Aunt," he said. "And I really need to see Sagal." Nurto laughed sarcastically. "You're grown up. You understand right from wrong."

When the sun had cooled down in the late afternoon, Liban and his father were sitting in front of the tent. "Father, I'm leaving for Mogadishu to see Sagal."

Sheik Omar shook his head and looked bitterly at Liban. "You can see this girl some other time. What is the rush at this time?" Liban and his father were at odds regarding the matter. Danger in the capital didn't seem to concern Liban, while his father saw the capital as a lethal place. There was a fire inside Liban. He was adamant about returning to the capital despite its perils.

Liban shoved two pants and one shirt in a small backpack.

His father said, "Maybe you're destined to die in Mogadishu."

"Please father, wish me good luck," Liban said.

"I wish you good luck."

Not many cars departed from Idag camp for Lamadhaafo. Liban was offered a ride by a white pickup driven by a man called Alidheere. Alidheere both smoked and chewed Qat, narcotic leaves chewed by many east African men. Liban had to pay him a transportation fee. As the pickup sped along, dust covered its four passengers, one of whom was a middle-aged woman. The passengers rarely spoke. It was as if they were afraid of each other.

At Lamadhaafo, Liban headed out to some houses he knew. Most of them were abandoned. He knocked on one gate and found an old woman. She was frail and sullen. Perhaps she couldn't flee, or something held her back. "Ayeeyo[1], how are you doing?" Liban asked.

"You see me. I'm here alone," she replied. "Where's your family?"

"They fled to Kenya. How long are you going to stay here?"

"God knows. Where are you from?" she asked.

"I'm originally from the capital but went to Kenya with my family. I'm coming back from there now," Liban said. He asked her if he

---

1 grandmother

could sleep there for the night. She agreed to his request. "What is your name?" he asked.

"I'm Foos," the woman answered. Before sunset, he toured some places in the town and saw that much had been abandoned. He concluded that what beautifies a town are its residents, not its buildings. He went to a number of bibitos[2] but couldn't find anyone who recognized him. He didn't know many people in Lamadhaafo, but he imagined he would recognize some.

He returned to Foos's house but had a restless sleep, preoccupied with thoughts of Sagal, getting a car to Mogadishu, his family in the refugee camp.

The following morning, Liban and Foos awoke to a clear sky and quiet town. It was empty except for armed militias, determined to defend the city from other militias. The armed Loodin militiamen screened anyone they suspected. As Liban looked for transportation to Mogadishu, he was now and then interrogated by them. He was asked about his lineage to make sure he wasn't a spy. Many years of sitting close to his father paid off. Liban had learned most of his clan information from overhearing his father talking with other people, so he knew his main clan and his subclan.

At noon, Liban found a minibus traveling to Mogadishu. The fare was very high, but he was obliged to pay it. The bus would leave at 5:30 p.m. so Liban hastened to Foos's house to collect his handbag. He bid goodbye to the elderly woman. At the bus station, there was a small eatery. He sat down on a small stool and asked to be served.

"We have rice and spaghetti, which one do you want?" a waiter asked.

"Get me a plate of rice," Liban said. Shortly after, he was handed a plate of rice topped with tomato sauce. He crossed his legs, slouched, and ate in haste. "Can I get a cup of water?" he asked and was handed a cup of water.

The bus honked to announce its imminent departure and Liban quickly finished his food, washed his hands, and left. He sat at a

---

2   cafés

window seat. Liban always liked widow seats, willing to pay extra, if necessary.

The bus was half empty. It seemed that people were afraid of going to the capital. Beside him sat a middle-aged man looking worried and pale. "Can you pushover a little bit?" he asked.

"Sure, I can," Liban said. He fidgeted, all the while looking at the man's face. The man frowned and tilted his head to a side. He must be a miserable man, Liban thought. Little conversation occurred among passengers. It was going to be a long night.

Early in the morning, the bus arrived in Mogadishu, dropping off every passenger at his or her neighbourhood. Liban got off in the Buulo-Yaray district. He shouldered his handbag and set out to Mustaf's house. Some people were still asleep because nobody went to school and nobody went to work anymore.

Liban knocked on the door of Mustaf's house. Shamsa, Mustaf's mother, came out. "Who's knocking?" she asked.

"It's me, Liban," he said. Shamsa opened the door.

She was shocked at seeing him.

"What brought you back here?" she asked.

"I came back to see the family," Liban answered.

"Sit down on that ganbar³," she told him. He sat down and collected himself.

"How's the neighbourhood, aunt?" he asked Shamsa, who was standing beside him.

"It's lonely. Many families have abandoned their homes."

"Is Mustaf asleep?"

"Mustaf doesn't live in Mogadishu anymore," Shamsa said.

Liban learned that Mustaf had gone to a distant town, afraid of being asked to join the militia. All able-bodied men of the Leexin were drafted to fight the Loodin clan.

Later, Muse, Mustaf's father, awoke. So did Sagal and Warsame, Mustaf's siblings. Upon hearing Sagal's voice, Liban sighed and smiled. Brushing her teeth with a soft wooden brush, she came and

---

3   stool

greeted him. "Asalamu Alaikum."

"Waalaikum salaam," he replied. Seeing Sagal was a big achievement and joy for him. For her sake, he had risked all that danger. He was burning with love. Sagal's parents knew that Liban had come for her. Nothing else.

Word spread that Liban Sheik was in the neighbourhood, so armed youths swarmed around Sagal's house. They knocked on the door.

"Is Liban here?" asked one militiaman.

Sagal's father came out, foaming.

"What do you want from us? It's not your business whether Liban is here or not," he said.

"We were told he's in your house. You must know that you're harbouring an enemy," one of the men said.

Muse didn't reply, lest his words escalate the situation. But nothing major took place. Liban didn't leave the house. The Muses treated him like royalty. Everyone was afraid, but Muse was armed and had military training. He wouldn't simply let the militiamen take Liban away from his sanctuary.

JANINE MUSTER

—

November Days

November hit the earth like a thunderstorm, loud and chaotic, a beautifully mean chaos. November, the month of grey-hearted skies, dead leaves, and the fresh smell of winter in the air. November brings an end to everything until the earth awakens again in the spring, when the first rays of sun finally hit the ground. A perfectly normal cycle.

"Weak language," is what he said, showing me that smirk, the way he always smirks when he tries to be funny, serious, offensive, and nice, all at once. I cannot resist that smile, his attitude always somewhat cryptic, his dark blonde hair never quite in place. Playfulness in his pale blue eyes but not without a hint of melancholy. Sipping my German beer and smoking one cigarette after another, I think about the meaning of his words, "weak language." He certainly has a point. If it was not for weak language, then things would have been different.

As the first day of November turns into the second, I can clearly hear the echo of his words, "weak language," still lingering, still confronting me. Someone I know very well calls. And I finally respond. He lives in a small town, in the East of Germany, almost 10,000 kilometers away. Far away from where I live now. All through October, he has been waiting patiently. Now he needs me to finally show signs of my existence. "Do you still want me to come in December?" is what he asks. "Yes! Yes, yes, yes. Please come now! Don't even wait until November is gone. Come, so we can sink deep into piles of blankets and pillows, bathe in hot chocolate, kiss and fuck. Don't hesitate! Don't waste November with your absence!" is what I wanted to say, is what I should have said. "I'm not sure," I say instead, unable to be clear, unable to make a decision.

It is already four o'clock in the morning. Confused talk and random thoughts. Ramblings of meaningless words. But not a word about him. Not a word about the way he draws me close to him and holds me tight when we embrace. Not a word about the way he makes me laugh when we spend time together. I know I need to say something. But I am not. I am not saying anything.

On the third day of November, I paint a gray wall white. Not noticing anything, I leave some ugly craters, no chance for repair, reflecting, maybe, what is happening inside, outside, around me. The dirt is gone. The wall now white. I look at the wall, thinking that it probably never was so white before. It makes those gashes all the more obvious and I have nothing that could cover them. I do not possess much.

Another long talk on the phone between night and morning, between the third and the fourth day of November. Some explanations. Some excuses. Trying to save. Trying to break. Trying to be honest with some lies. I do not tell him that it is not he whom I miss when I am at work.

When I am at work I think about those pale blue eyes making me feel like leaves dancing in the soft wind held only by the warm sun. When I am at work I think about this warm, deep voice making me feel like a bonfire joyfully crackling during a mild summer night.

What I finally tell him is that I feel drawn to those eyes, this voice. "But it doesn't mean a lot," I lie. "We are only roommates," I add. "Not much has happened," I reassure him, still using weak language.

I smile as I remember those kisses walking hand in hand across the field. The dry, sweet fragrance of hay still lingering in my nose. Luckily, he cannot see me smile.

"Why did you have to go to Canada?" he complains. His voice, now somewhat high-pitched and unpleasant, immediately annoys me. It annoys me almost more than his question does. "Because I've never been anywhere. I always wanted to play somewhere else. You knew that." "Yes. I guess. I just didn't think you would actually go," he says. "Besides, Edmonton is not New York." It was this subtle arrogance that once drew me to him.

"How do you know that? You've never been here," I defend my choice. "No, I haven't. But nobody here has ever heard of this orchestra," he defends himself. "I still care for you and I will be back soon," I say and hang up the phone before he can mention December again.

It was on a warm day in mid-May during a Baroque music festival almost three years ago when we first met, when the clouds were shaped like heads of cauliflowers, when the shadows playfully moved through the cobblestoned courtyards, when those East German villages still felt like home. In the safety of the castle's Romanesque towers, I played oboe da caccia, a rather awkward-looking instrument, in front of a small audience.

He approached me afterwards. "Did you know that it was Bach who inspired the creation of that instrument, its curved tube and brass bell?" he asked. "I am just asking because musicians like you often don't know anything about the instruments they are playing." "That's quite an assumption," I responded. "You won't find anybody here who doesn't know everything about their instruments. Here, everyone loves and knows Baroque. Who are you again?"

He told me that he studied the history of Baroque instruments, that he was writing his dissertation on Bach and his use of oboes, that he would soon be a music historian. "And you couldn't think of a more interesting fact about oboes to impress me?" Instead of responding, he laughed awkwardly and shrugged his shoulders, gestures I found endearing at the time.

No longer interested in challenging my knowledge about oboes, he asked me if I only played Baroque music in small East German villages. "For now, yes. But I would like to play in great orchestras. In Berlin, London, Sydney, New York. I would love to play in New York." He nodded. And I wondered how he could survive the sun in his grey tweed suit. He did not take off his blazer. He made no attempts to roll up the sleeves of his black turtleneck. We were standing in the castle's courtyard in the midst of a masking scent. Permeating through the windless air, the odour of his sunscreen made it impossible to catch the fragrance of the flowers that surrounded us.

It was on a cloudless night in late June when he asked me to move in with him, when we played hide and seek underneath the starry sky, when we were drinking glass after glass of red wine, when we were listening to nothing but Bach. I was not sure. But his decisiveness impressed me, his determination drew me to him.

I moved in with him on a Sunday in early July. Moving did not take long. I did not possess much. But in the midst of July's stagnant air, the sweat was still dripping off our foreheads.

The days that followed were bright and hot. We stayed cool inside and talked about Bach and his use of oboes. I played oboe for him. We read books to each other, discussed Schopenhauer's philosophy, and drank cups of iced tea. We stayed cool inside because he does not like the sun. He does not like lying in the green grass, walking along the shore lines of those azure blue lakes, burying his toes in the soft, warm sand. In his presence, I forgot that I once liked the sun. I forgot about the grass, the lakes, the sand.

In the gloominess of mid-August rain, he started to leave town often. He left town for most of August and for most of the months that followed. He travelled to Berlin, London, Sydney, New York. He spent weeks at those places to talk to people about Bach's use of oboes. While he was gone I stayed at home, playing the oboe for myself, missing his remarks on how I could improve my posture, my embouchure, my tone. I usually laughed at his comments. He does not know how to play oboe.

When he came back, he told me that Berlin was too pretentious, that London was too expensive, that Sydney was too hot, that New York was too busy. It seemed as if he did not want me to go there myself. Not because he did not want me to see other places. But because he was scared of losing me to them. I still could not help but to admire his dedication to music history and his courage in going, seeing, experiencing something new.

Fall was short that year and winter cold. January, February, March passed slowly. I discovered that he did not appreciate my love for Wagner's *Tristan and Isolde*, that he did not like the way I dressed when I did not perform, that he did not like that I smoked much. But he still bought me a black marble ashtray, square and heavy. He placed it on the white picnic table, outside on our balcony. The sun came back in April. And I spent hours on this balcony, smoking cigarette after cigarette, unable to stop thinking about playing in Berlin, London, Sydney, New York one day.

On the fifth day of November, I receive a letter. It comes from far away, has travelled 10,000 kilometers. He must have sent it a while ago. He must have felt something for some time. His handwriting—I can picture his yellow-green fountain pen with its thin nib—shows signs of sadness, does not look as determined as it usually does. I still can picture the decisiveness in his green eyes, his auburn hair never out of place. His strong arms always capable of lifting me, swirling me through the air. His fair skin never without sunscreen. His face with its million freckles.

I had tried to count them one day. I had tried to count them while we were waiting for the train to bring us to one of those East German villages. I was nervous about my performance and he was supposed to meet important people who know much about Bach. I did not want him to come with me. I did not want him to miss his chance to talk to those people. But he insisted. He chose to come to my performance instead of meeting with them. During the train ride he reassured me that I would master the middle movement of Bach's concerto for oboe and violin. He had heard me play it perfectly before. Counting his freckles made me feel calm. His presence made me feel secure. His reassurance made me feel confident. My performance went incredibly well that day.

In his letter he writes about the time when he first knew that he only wanted to be with me. He remembers the smell of peppermint tea, the rain against our living room window. I remember it too. I remember sitting close to him in our brown-cushioned chair, rocking back and forth, reading Nietzsche's *The Birth of Tragedy* while he wrote page after page about Bach's use of oboes. The quiet sound of the keys, the floor cracking under the chair, the rustling sound of the pages turning. It made for a comforting space, a space in which only we existed, a space in which we only needed each other.

In his letter he tells me that he cannot imagine that such comfort is possible with somebody else, that he cannot picture a different woman sitting next to him rocking back and forth in this brown-cushioned chair. He does not want our relationship to end. And in the moment of reading his letter, I do not want our relationship to end either. But I start to think that feeling comfortable is not a good reason for being with someone.

What then is a good reason for being with someone, I ask myself while sitting outside. Smoking one cigarette after another, I no longer think about the letter and the one who wrote it. Instead, I think about the playfulness in those pale blue eyes, the warmth of that deep voice, our dream of going to Hawaii. Soon after we met, we discovered that we liked each other and started to dream beautiful but hopeless dreams. Hopeless because I could feel his uncertainty, his fear of going, of seeing, of experiencing something new, his anxiety at not yet knowing the meaning and purpose of his life. Although still uncertain, I no longer share that fear, that anxiety. I am closer than him to knowing the meaning and purpose of mine. But thinking about the time when we first started to like each other, I catch myself smile.

It was in late September when I first thought I could like him, when the alleyways only belonged to us, when the sky turned mustard yellow and the sun hid behind those heavy clouds, when the wind carefully rocked the coloured leaves. We climbed into the dumpsters and bathed in strangers' filth, not looking for anything specific. We found an old photo album of a young man unknown to us. Stories emerged from those pictures.

The young man's vacation in Hawaii surrounded by his friends, pictures that showed us a place filled with palm trees and beaches. People laughing and screaming as they run towards the water. Waves crashing against volcanic rock. A place that calls for walking along those elegantly curved shore lines, for playing in the azure blue ocean, for burying toes in the soft, warm sand, for climbing the dark volcanic rock. Hawaii. There also were pictures of the young man biking through streets of towns we did not recognize. We shared this lack of having traveled. We laughed because there still was time. There still was time to catch up with the young man in those photographs, to bike through unfamiliar streets of not yet discovered towns. But looking into his eyes, I could see fear taking over. I saw my own fear reflected in his eyes. But unlike him, I was ready to go somewhere unfamiliar, ready to explore something new.

I smiled as I looked at pictures of the young man graduating from university, receiving his degree. I thought about my own graduation. It felt good to finally be a professional musician. On the day I received my degree, I knew that I would be able eventually to play wherever I wanted. Standing inside the dumpster, the mustard yellow clouds above me, the young man's photo album in my hand, I knew that I was not far away from playing in big orchestras; I was no longer nervous about my performances. I turned to him and saw that melancholy was growing in his eyes, overshadowing their playfulness once again. He seemed to be scared, scared of finishing his degree, uncertain of how a philosopher could fit in this world. I saw my own uncertainty reflected in his eyes. But unlike him, I was no longer scared. I knew how an oboist would fit into this world.

Looking at a picture of the young man and his lover, lying arm in arm in the green grass, we wished we could lie in the green grass too. I could feel his eyes on me as I climbed out of the dumpster.

In the comfort of September's rain, we started to wear each other's clothes. My sand-washed jeans with holes in both knees fit him perfectly. His button-down flannel shirt with its blue and red squares fit me perfectly. He liked the way I dressed when I did not perform.

He also liked that I smoke much. On the nights I did not perform, we sat side by side on our patio. Smoking one cigarette after another, we dreamt about going to Hawaii one day.

It was early in October when I first knew I liked him, when I left town over the weekend to get some distance, when I realized, while I was gone, how much I missed him, when I longed for nothing more but to be with him. The bus ride back to him felt longer.

When I got back, we started to sleep in each other's beds. We lay side by side, careful not to touch. I could still feel his body through the walls of blankets and pillows. His distinct scent in my nose, his quiet breath in my ears. It made for sleepless nights. We hugged and we kissed, but only from the distance, only with our eyes.

It was in the golden glow of a Sunday in mid-October when we kissed first. One kiss followed by others. Walking towards the edge of the field, he found my hand. His hand felt warm in mine. I pressed it hard, knowing that we would not be able to stay like that. He sighed, his face now close to mine. I caught a fragrance of cut hay, dry and sweet. Walking hand in hand across the field, we were able to forget about reality.

On that day, our boundary broke. We now hugged and kissed. With our bodies unable to stay apart, we could not resist touching. But only when nobody else was around. The people we lived with knew I was not free.

It was in late October when we were lying on the black leather couch in our living room, holding each other. He moved his fingers softly through my hair while my body shivered under his gentle motions. "Eventually the season will end and I will have to leave.

Back to Germany. Back to him," I said. His eyes, now imitating mine, grew melancholic.

He moved his hand to grab a cigarette. "You haven't said anything to him yet?" he asked, playing with the cigarette between his fingers. "No," I answered. "We don't sleep with each other. We only sleep next to each other. So far, there is not much to tell. Not much has happened." I took the cigarette out of his hand, rolling it between my fingers now. "I'm not sure if I can leave him. I care for him. And I'm scared."

He did not ask if I could stay with him. He did not ask if he could come with me. He did not ask why I was scared. "Not much has happened," he repeated instead, while his mind seemed to be elsewhere.

A second later, his eyes darted back to meet mine. "Weak language," he suddenly said, showing me that smirk, the way he always smirks when he tries to be funny, serious, offensive, and nice, all at once. I cannot resist that smile, his attitude always somewhat cryptic, his dark blonde hair never quite in place. Playfulness in his pale blue eyes but not without a hint of melancholy. "I know," I said. And then, not quite yet able to fathom the weight behind his words, I lit the cigarette.

In the evening of the sixth day of November, I sit outside waiting for him to finally come back from university. I catch myself thinking about the meaning of his words, "weak language." I wonder if I use weak language as a strategy, as a way that allows me to escape my decision-making.

He finally comes home and does not behave differently than on all the other days that he came home, skipping, jumping, joking, drowning our secret in humor. It often works. Of course, there are days when his method fails me, but I usually lose confusion looking into his eyes, those eyes. He now gets confused looking into mine.

He still follows our usual routine, gracefully and smoothly. We are like a well-rehearsed dance. After skipping, jumping, and joking, after drowning our secret in humour, and after everyone we live

with has gone to bed, he draws me close to him, holds me long and
tight, and asks me, softly whispering into my ear, how my day was. I
follow his lead, not yet willing to break our routine either.

Sitting close to him on the black leather couch in our living room,
I tell him about my practice with the orchestra. And as I normally
would, I impersonate the conductor, a tall man with black hair and
horn-rimmed glasses. He makes good use of his baton, swinging it
through the air with profound intensity. And as he normally would,
he laughs with me when I use my arms trying to swing my invisible
baton, and when I use all of my face muscles trying to look as intense
as my conductor does shortly before the orchestra starts playing
Mahler's 2nd symphony.

After my performance, he proceeds with our usual routine by
telling me about his favourite philosophy course, imitating his professor. He first ruffles his hair, making it stick up even more. He then
raises his right index finger and says, in the lowest, deepest voice he
can muster, "Nietzsche and Wagner bonded over their love for Schopenhauer's philosophy. They even wrote letters to each other, back
and forth, for years. But don't be fooled. They weren't friends. They
only used each other, being the self-absorbed geniuses they were."
And as I normally do, I laugh with him when he shares with me some
of his professor's remarks. "You should come to our course one day.
You can talk about Wagner and how he brings Schopenhauer's philosophy to life in *Tristan and Isolde*. Dr Rose would like that. He is
always looking for guest lecturers. And I know how much you love
that opera." "Yes, that would be fun," I agree. "As long as I don't
have to talk about Bach."

We look at each other knowing that we can no longer follow our
usual routine, where one of us will get up and take the other's hand.
We will then go to one of our rooms; sometimes his, sometimes mine,
and fall asleep next to each other. But not today.

"You talked to him, didn't you?" "No. But yesterday I got a letter
from him. Reading his letter made me miss him. I'm still not sure if I
should stay with him. Leaving him would hurt him but staying with

him would hurt you." "You don't need to worry about me. I always knew you weren't free. I thought I would have this secret crush on you until you leave. But now . . . " "But now what?"

Instead of responding, he turns away, which is his usual way of escaping conversations, of leaving questions unanswered. We are too similar, I think to myself. We both are indecisive, unable to make decisions.

He seems far away and I cannot grasp what he is thinking. While his mind seems to be elsewhere, my thoughts start to drift as well. I imagine myself performing in Wagner's operas in Berlin, London, Sydney, New York instead of playing Bach's chamber music in small East German villages; the thought makes me smile. I wonder if it would be best for us to stop spending so much time together. Being with him might distract me from fulfilling my dreams. Being with me might distract him from finding his. I do not want him to come with me to Berlin, London, Sydney, New York if these are not the places he wants to see. And I do not want to stay here and wait for him until he knows where he wants to go.

"We shouldn't spend so much time together," I finally break the silence. Instead of disagreeing, he holds me tight, his arms around me. "This is not me trying not to cry. This is me, trying to cry. I want my tears to evaporate yours," he says.

I wake up alone on the seventh day of November. We did not share a bed this night, this night when he tried to evaporate my tears with his. My room feels empty without him lying next to me, even emptier than it already is. I look at the wall's ugly craters. They are more obvious today than on other days. I go to orchestra practice wearing my own clothes.

The eighth, ninth, and tenth day of November are foggy, blur together. We have not talked since the night I broke away from him. He stays out longer now. When he comes home, he does not skip, jump, joke. No attempts to drown our secret in humor. His eyes,

although still pale blue, are no longer those eyes, are no longer playful. I have seen him a million times while walking through the streets
these days. But it was never him.

I need to respond to the letter too. I need to be clear for once.
But with November's dullness around, I am still not able to make a
decision.

On the eleventh day of November, I come home from work and,
to my surprise, find the house filled with people. Some of them are
familiar, but some of them I do not recognize. I spot him right away,
sitting on the large picnic table in the living room surrounded by
friends. In his laughter, slightly louder than it normally is and somewhat obnoxious, I can see that he is only pretending. I am certain that
nobody else recognizes these subtle differences. I know him well.

He notices me as soon as I enter the room. I talk to people on the
side that is furthest away from him, hoping that there is enough space
between us. But as I look up, I meet his eyes. And they are those eyes
again, hugging and kissing me from the distance. A slight motion
of his head tells me that he wants me to come with him. He leaves
the party and, after a slight delay, I follow him. Entering his room, I
realize how much I have missed being here, in this space, in his space,
filled with books by great writers and existential philosophers like
Nietzsche, Sartre, Camus, CDs of local punk rock bands, paintings of
flowers and cats, and all sorts of strangely shaped figurines that speak
to both his playfulness and melancholy. I think about how he often
seems detached from the world around him and how he often seems
he can only escape this emptiness within play. I become uncertain,
scared of being nothing but a character in his tragic drama, scared of
him being nothing but a character in mine.

We do not say anything. We only kiss and hold each other. Clumsily, he begins to pull the sweater over my head; uncertainty in his
eyes. Certain for once, I let it happen. I had longed for nothing more
but to be close to him. Opening the buttons of my sand-washed
jeans with holes in both knees, his certainty grows. Clumsily, I begin

to unbutton his flannel shirt with its blue and red squares. Seeing him without clothes confirms what I had already felt holding him, embracing him. We are both thin, not eating much of anything. Bones stick out and I can see his ribs. Feeling the warmth of his body and the softness of his skin, I become uncertain again. We share too much. I have my own collection of strangely shaped figurines in the house where I grew up. I have my own collection of books written by existential philosophers.

I feel troubled for being with him now, for not having written the letter first, for hardly remembering Germany. But as his lips touch mine, I lose all my thoughts.

We are holding onto each other, while we sink deep into the pile of blankets and pillows. "Tell me again what you see in him?" I wonder why he does not ask me what I see in him instead. "I see familiarity," I say as I turn away from him. What I should have added is that I see someone who would, if I slipped and fell into a river, jump after me without hesitation and would be strong enough to save me from drowning. I also see someone who knows what he wants and is capable of fulfilling his dreams. Things I do not see in him.

"You should leave the both of us," he finally says while I move my fingers softly through his hair. "Him, because I like you more than I should. And me, because I'm selfish for wanting you all to myself." Wanting me all to himself, I think as I move my hand to grab a cigarette. He must know that he is not selfish for wanting me all to himself. But he does not suggest any other possibilities. And I do not ask him if he can picture a future in which we are together. The thought of playing in big orchestras crosses my mind again. I think about doing what I desire without having to take somebody else into account and get excited. "I know," I agree, rolling the cigarette between my fingers, "and I probably will. But for different reasons." He takes the cigarette out of my hand, rolling it between his fingers now.

"It is still November and you are still here," he says. There is that smirk again, the way he always smirks when he tries to be funny, serious, offensive, and nice, all at once. I hope I can resist that smile, his attitude always somewhat cryptic, his dark blonde hair never quite in place. Playfulness in his pale blue eyes but not without a hint of melancholy. And then, not quite yet able to fathom the weight behind my words, he lights the cigarette.

drama.

AKSAM ALYOUSEF

—ᴐ

Hagar

Background

In 2012, Aleppo, the economic capital of Syria, fell into the hands of
a number of militant Islamic factions. Once they took control of most
of the city's neighbourhoods, the battles began, which made civilian
existence a living hell.

Characters

Hagar: a Syrian woman in her thirties.
Nazeer: a Syrian man, 45, a friend of Hagar's ex-husband.

Setting

A simply furnished home in Aleppo in the present day. Events take
place between the first and second birthdays of Hagar's son, Jamal,
2014-2015.

On the left side of the stage is Jamal's crib. There is a rocking chair, a table and a couch. Four chairs surround the table. On the table is a birthday cake with two candles. Six sandbags are placed up against a covered window in the room. A film screen covers a large part of the rear of the stage.

An imaginary line separates the left and right halves of the stage. The right side is a mirror image of the left side, except that the lighting is brighter on the right side. The only difference is that the cake has one candle, not two. Otherwise the right-side set is the same as the left side.

Hagar is seated in the left side rocking chair, holding Jamal in her arms, who is wrapped in a wool blanket. She is wearing a scarf on her head.

At sunrise:

HAGAR: *(singing to Jamal)*
   O sea, for the sake of your waves
   Don't disturb those who sleep
   O sea, for the sake of your tides
   Ebb quietly, lest you wake tender hearts
   O sea, who ṣets up your waves
   As a swing for the moon
   O sea, who sets up your waves
   My dreams have been lost
   And my wounds are laid bare to the waters.

Hagar rises from the rocking chair (with Jamal) and goes over the imaginary line to the right side of the stage. Jamal starts to cry. The crying stops and Hagar puts Jamal in his crib. She picks up her cell phone from the table and dials a number.

HAGAR: *(talking to herself while she dials)*
Let's see what's the matter with this man . . .

Hello, Mr Abouarif, how are you? It's like you hear on the news. It's worse everyday . . .

I'm almost ready . . . No, no, no, I'll be ready by Friday, God willing.

What? . . . Why from Mersin? . . . We agreed it's better to leave from Izmir. We should stick to the plan. I have a baby. I don't want the sea journey to be too

Long . . .

No, never, I don't know anyone in Mersin. Everyone says it's better to leave from Izmir . . .

The money? I have $1500. Don't worry, I will get the rest by Friday. I'll call you back when I get the rest.

Yah.

Thank you. Goodbye.

> *Hagar ends the call. Machine gun fire starts up outside. Hagar, looking scared, runs to her son's crib. She pulls the crib near to the window where the sandbags are placed. She sits down beside the crib under the window. She speaks to Jamal in a low, comforting voice.*

Don't worry, my baby, don't worry. We'll be leaving in a few days. We'll make it to Europe and get away from all this . . .

> *The gunfire stops. Hagar, as if addressing the gunfire.*

I hope God destroys you. Don't you get tired of all this? You've made us hate life.

HAGAR: *(speaking to Jamal)*

I envy you. You don't know what is happening. It makes me feel better that you don't know what fear means. I don't ever want you to feel fear. Come on, wake up, little one! Let's celebrate your birthday and blow out the candle . . .

It's not fair that I have to have your birthday alone . . . I know it's not a time to celebrate. But, what can I do? I can't ignore your first birthday. If there was no war, I would have a real party, with decorations, a feast for all the family and friends and we would shower you with gifts.

Hagar grabs a broom and starts sweeping the floor around the sandbar.

HAGAR: *(looks lovingly at Jamal)*

Oh, my sweet boy, you're just like an angel. Sleep—I can't disturb you. You wake when you want. I will just wait. I have nothing else to do . . . except clean up after this fucking sandbag. *(She angrily addresses a leaking sandbag.)* I'm always cleaning up after you. I'm so tired of you. I pray for the day when I throw you out of my home.

We hear a huge explosion which appears to rock the set.

Oh my God!

She goes to the sandbags and crouches down beside them. She touches one of the sandbags, addressing it.

I'm sorry! Please make as much mess as you like. In fact, you entertain me, because without you I have nothing to do.

And you are the only ones that care about us . . . you protect us from the bullets.

I'd like to invite you to my son's birthday party.

She goes to the crib and whispers.

We have visitors now.

Again, addressing the sandbags.

Look, let's make a deal. You can't leave the window all at the same time. Only three of you can come to the table at once. Then you will make way for the other three. Does that sound good? I will make the necessary arrangements.

She picks up the first sandbag and places it on one of the chairs, speaking to it.

Your name is Mahmoud.

She picks up a second sandbag and puts it on another chair.

Your name is Firas.

She picks up a third sandbag, which is tied with red tape, and puts it on a third chair.

And you, beautiful lady, I will call you Randa.

She returns to the three remaining sandbags.

And you are Ghyath and you Ghith and you, Rami.

She brings dishes and glasses and puts them on the table.

You are all welcome. I'm so glad you could make it. Oh, I forgot the forks.

She collects forks and puts them on the table.

HAGAR: *(talking to the sandbags)*

Really, I am so happy you're here—I couldn't even invite the neighbours. You know, since the kidnappings and sniper fire began, no one will leave their homes, except for an emergency. And anyway, most homes have been abandoned now. There's just a few people who haven't been able to leave yet, and a few so wretched that they've given up all hope, here, there or anywhere.

It wouldn't be right to invite the Aboujafir family when their son's blood is still warm. God bless his soul! He was such a beautiful boy, just 10 years old. I don't understand why a suicide bomber would target an elementary school. Why? What do they want?

She gets more and more emotional.

Oh my God! His mother had to pick up what was left of him.

She tries to calm herself down.

I couldn't invite the Aboumoner family. Their daughter was kidnapped 6 months ago. Even now, they have no idea what happened . . . She left for work and never came back. Her father has aged 20 years in six months. The poor girl—God knows what they did to her.

She is feeling guilty talking to herself. She turns to the crib and talks to Jamal.

Do you think it's right to have a party? I think it's okay— it's your first birthday. Life has to go on. That's what they keep telling us on TV every day.

She arranges a place setting in front of each sandbag. She shyly avoids looking directly at the sandbags, as if they were real guests.

HAGAR: *(whispering to the sandbags)*
We are having this party in secret. No one knows about it, just you and me. *(To Jamal)* Oh Jamal, I don't know. It would have been better if you came earlier—or later. I wish you had waited until this war was over. Then you would have had a house without sandbags at the window, a house with light streaming in through your window. You would have had a school, garden, park, not these stray bullets and car bombs.

I know this trip will be humiliating. But what can we do? Anyway, you are still young and you won't feel anything too unusual. But I will. But that's not a problem. I'm ready to be humiliated all my life if it is to make you safe. God forgive your father! Life is so lonely for me. If your father was here, this trip would be easier.

HAGAR: *(talking to herself)*
But maybe nothing bad will happen. Most people I know have arrived in Europe without any real problems.

HAGAR: *(to the sandbags)*
What do these countries have to lose by giving us visas? If they gave us visas, we could all avoid risking our lives to cross the sea. We are all leaving anyway. Why are they willing to see us drown?

She adopts a mocking tone of voice.

And they talk about human rights! They don't see us as human, just as numbers. Numbers of refugees, numbers of murders, numbers of injured, kidnapped, raped.

She picks up an old newspaper and starts reading the headline.

"Thirty-five murdered in bus explosion."

She pretends she is a Western reader.

Thirty-five is a big number! Oh, the poor families! Those goddamn terrorists! It's a shame—honey, can you pour me some more tea?

She closes the newspaper.

Then we are forgotten—nameless, endless victims with a teaspoonful of sympathy. How can people there imagine the face of just one mother whose sees her child murdered? Who can bear to feel the anguish of love and hope extinguished in a second. Who would this child have been? A doctor, an engineer, a lawyer, maybe a garbage collector. Now, felled by a stray bullet, they're prey for the powerful, the dogs of war.

Shooting starts outside. HAGAR keeps quiet for a moment, until the shooting stops.

HAGAR: *(addressing a sandbag)*
Look, Mr Mahmoud, you should remember something very important. If these monsters had not been unleashed on our land, this war would never have happened. And now the whole world is involved. Oh, they say this war is for our benefit and will bring peace, freedom and dignity! They are lying. Every country involved in this war has something to gain. No one cares how many of us are killed. If they really cared about us, they wouldn't close the borders to keep us out. As if we were the enemy!

We Syrians have no choices. We are in the theatre of war

and there's no exit. We're forced to kill or be killed. I don't want my son to kill or be killed. He has the right to grow up and study. And I have the right to see him on the corner of the street waiting for a beautiful girl. He will smile at her and she'll pretend to be shy. I want him to fall in love and get married and then to make jokes with his friends about married life!

I want my son to come to me and complain about his wife's demands, and then go home in the evening and hug her and say how much he loves her. It's alright for him to complain to me about his wife because I know only half of it is true. The next day I will go to his wife and tease her about my son's complaints. He will pretend to be the victim, caught between his mother and his wife. I just want my son to live.

I have the right to decorate this cake with two candles, or three or ten or fifty. When people ask me about him, I'll say the more he grows, the more I worry more about him—just like every mother.

HAGAR: *(feeling helpless)*

I want to leave here just so I can survive. *(she controls herself)* I'd start my life again. I'd give up everything for him. I'd leave my dreams hidden in every corner of this house. I would forget my own language, my education and my history . . . What use is a degree in history? If I had known what was going to happen, I would have studied something useful—like English, or technology, or nursing. What use is the history of Syria now? *(laughing)*

What a stupid saying: "History repeats itself." History doesn't repeat itself, we are just fools who never learn and are condemned to keep making the same mistakes.

She feels that she is chattering too much, so she stops.

I think he should wake up. He should have slept enough. What kind of birthday party is this, where the birthday boy is asleep? Excuse me a minute. I'll see if he's ready to wake up.

She moves toward the crib located on the left side.

HAGAR: *(to her son)*
Come on, wake up.

> *She remembers something. She runs to the sand bags. She carries three of them and puts them on the chairs. Then she returns to her son.*

Come on, wake up. It's not polite to sleep when we have guests.

She looks at her son's face.

My God! You're so beautiful! You are an angel, you know that? Wake up for a little, then you can go back to sleep. Just for ten minutes, so I can look into your eyes and see your smile. You don't want to wake up do you? That's ok; I won't sleep until you wake up. It's been a long time since I slept. You've stolen the sleep from my eyes. I'm sorry, my sweet, for what happened. I did it all for you. I did it so you could live without fear. I didn't bring you into this world to die young, my darling. When you were born, death was everywhere. I was afraid that I would lose you at any moment. Even when you were sleeping in your crib, I was afraid that a shell would land on you and take you from me.

It's true that death can come to anyone, at any time and any place. But the chance of you meeting death in this place was so much greater. That's why I ran away with you, so we could live in a place where death does not prowl around every corner.

Her cell phone rings and she looks at the number.
She decides not to answer it.

HAGAR: *(to herself)*

Oh—why now? No, not now! I never want to speak to you
again. We are done! I don't want anything from you. Go
away and be with your new wife. I don't want to hear your
voice. You abandoned us when we needed you. If you had
stayed with us, maybe none of this would have happened.

Goes to her son and picks him up.

I'm sorry, my love. I know you are sleeping and comfortable,
but what can I do? I miss you when you are not in my arms.
Sleep, sleep, that's okay. Don't they say a child sleeps the
sweetest in his mother's arms? Come, come, let me hold you
for a while.

She picks him up and walks with him while she is
talking.

My love, let me tell you a story. I know you can't hear it but, I
want to keep busy. I'm sorry, but what else is there to do? It's
not "Little Red Riding Hood." That's far too tame. We don't
need to go down to the woods, now the wolves are all around
us. "Cinderella" is a very beautiful story . . . but I want to
tell you about chivalry and men of great honour. They are
so rare now. Your grandfather was a great man. If he said or
promised he would do something, he would do it, even if it
cost him his life. He never took advantage of anyone—and
he would stand of the way of anyone who tried. He would
actually look for people in need and help them.

She walks to the right side of the stage.

It wasn't just your grandfather . . . many people were like
him.

As soon as she crosses the imaginary line, the phone rings.

One minute. Let me answer the phone.

She puts him in his crib and grabs her phone and answers it.

Yes, Abouarif?

Yes, I can hear you.

What's changed?

What are you saying, Abouarif?

Did we not agree on $2000?

Why are you changing it now?

Abouarif, we started with $800, and every time, you tell me the price has gone up.

Yes, I care about the quality of the boat . . .

Of course, safety is very important, but $3500 is too much.

You need to understand my situation.

I am collecting money from here and there, tiny amounts.

If the price gets higher, I just won't be able to go.

Alright, what can I do?

I can't pay another dollar over $3500.

Alright, no problem.

Thank you. Goodbye.

She hangs up.

What a son of a bitch! Thief! Bastard bloodsucker!

She throws the phone on the couch.

How am I going to get the rest of the money? There's no one left. The only option is Nazeer. He said to call if I needed anything.

She holds the phone as if to call, but she changes her mind.

Only this fucking war is making me do this.

She throws the phone back on the couch.

It's so hard to ask for help.

She goes to her son's crib and picks him up again.

I have to call him. I have nothing to lose.

She starts looking for Nazeer's name in her cellphone contacts list, and then she calls him. We hear the phone ring. The phone screen appears on the screen that is set up in the rear of the stage.

HAGAR:
Hi Nazeer.

NAZEER: *(joyfully)*
Hi Hagar, how are you?

HAGAR:
I am good, what about you?

NAZEER:
Turn on the camera so I can see you.

HAGAR:

We are talking Nazeer, we don't need a camera.

NAZEER:

Go on, sweetheart, turn it on. What have you got to lose?

HAGAR:

OK, Nazeer, as you like.

> *She turns the camera on, then we can see Nazeer on the stage screen.*

NAZEER:

Wow Hagar! Beautiful as always. How long has it been since we've seen each other?

HAGAR:

How are your wife and kids?

NAZEER:

They're all well. What's going on with you? You haven't called for a long time.

HAGAR:

It's hard here. We have electricity for a day, and then we don't have it for ten days. We have the internet for a day, and then we don't have it for a month. Anyway, how is work? How's life in Dubai?

NAZEER:

Everything is good. You know, Syrians always succeed. We're smart people.

HAGAR: *(mocking)*

Yeah, we're so smart! Come and see what's become of our country. We're so smart.

NAZEER:

> Syria will recover.

HAGAR:

> Not if we don't stop this madness. Nazeer, it's getting worse here every day. But I don't want to talk about it. Tell me, what are you doing there now?

NAZEER:

> I have a restaurant in downtown Dubai. It's doing fantastically. People here love Syrian food.

HAGAR:

> Perfect. That's good news. Congratulations! Look, I know you're very busy, so I won't waste your time. I need something from you.

NAZEER:

> I always have time for you, Hagar. And you can ask me anything.

HAGAR:

> Thank you Nazeer. I have decided to leave Syria. It's so bad here. I am going to go to Turkey, then from Turkey to Germany or Sweden.

NAZEER:

> I don't understand why you haven't left already.

HAGAR:

> It's the money, Nazeer. The journey costs $3,500. I only have $2,000. So, can you lend me $1500? I will give it back to you when I have a job there. Is that possible?

NAZEER:

> For sure, when do you want it?

HAGAR:

As soon as possible. I plan to leave next Friday.

NAZEER:

That's okay. The exchange companies are closed now—it's 10 p.m. here. Tomorrow morning I'll send you the money.

HAGAR:

I really appreciate that, thank you so much Nazeer.

NAZEER:

You are very welcome, Hagar. You know what you mean to me.

HAGAR:

I know, I know.

NAZEER:

I heard that your husband got married to another woman. Is it true?

HAGAR:

Are there no secrets left in the world?

NAZEER:

What happened? Tell me.

HAGAR:

There's not much to say. Five months ago, he went to Damascus to look for a job, and he didn't come back.

NAZEER:

So, now you are alone.

HAGAR:

No. My baby is here. Today is his first birthday.

NAZEER:

Really? Happy Birthday to him.

HAGAR:

Thank you.

Nazeer looks at her in a sleazy, lustful way.

NAZEER:

You know I miss you, Hagar.

HAGAR:

Please Nazeer, don't start.

NAZEER:

Don't be mean.

HAGAR:

Nazeer, you are my husband's best friend. You are married and have children. I do too.

NAZEER:

Your husband left you and married another woman.

HAGAR:

It is not about him. It is about me.

She feels uncomfortable and wants to hang up.

HAGAR:

Nazeer, when you send me the money, please message me to say when I can pick it up.

Nazeer feels bitter because she didn't respond to his flirting.

NAZEER:

Hang on, I just remembered. I can't send you the money tomorrow. I have an important meeting in Sharjah and I need to leave really early.

HAGAR:

No problem, you can send it the day after.

NAZEER:

I have to stay in Sharjah for a week. Can you wait?

HAGAR:

I need it by Friday. Don't worry, I'll find someone else to help me.

NAZEER:

Okay. Hagar, keep in touch. Take care. Bye.

HAGAR:

Bye.

She hangs up and spits at the phone.

HAGAR:

Bastard! All you men are bastards. I can't believe . . .

We hear a heavy mortar shell exploding. Hagar is really scared as it seems so close. Jamal starts crying.

HAGAR:

God, help us!

Another shell explodes. She runs to Jamal and grabs him from the crib.

Lights go dark. Lights turn up. Hagar is sitting on a chair on the left side of the stage. Jamal is in his crib.

HAGAR:

Nothing has changed. We went and came back and it's as if

we never left. The only thing that has not come back is our lives. This place that we ran away from was more merciful than any other place. I wish we had never left. Here, I had lots of dreams for your future. I took you and we followed our dream. Sadly, this dream was a nightmare.

When I was young, my dad took me to Lebanon to visit some relatives. My dad's work here was unstable, so our relatives suggested that he work with them. Even though Lebanon is right next door and is very similar I felt like I didn't want to live anywhere but here. This place is not like any place in the world. Not because it is the best place, but because it is my place. Everything that happens in this place, belongs to me. This sand is mine. The eyes of strangers that look at me through the window are mine. Even the hands that try to grope me on the bus are mine! People would describe the West as being like heaven, but I never felt the need to move. Those countries are not ours. Our place is here. And nothing equals the feeling that your roots are deep in your own ground.

It is hard for us to establish roots in other countries. Maybe our kids can put down their roots in the new place. But not us. So no matter what happens, we will always be foreigners. We won't be happy. Only here at home can we make our own heaven. Our real heaven is here, so why did we make it into hell?

> *She stands by the window, like she is talking to someone.*

No, I don't want to travel. I want to stay here no matter what. I have imagined everything that could happen here, but I never imagined a time when we would kill each other. Even when we started killing each other, I never thought of leaving. Death here is better than being a refugee.

HAGAR: *(to her son)*

But when you came everything changed. I could never imagine anything happening to you. Your life was my responsibility. I have no right to risk it. I wanted to protect you.

She feels ashamed.

That's why I did what I shouldn't have done.

Lighting turns to black.

Lighting returns. She is on the right side of the stage, talking with Nazeer. Nazeer appears on the screen while Hagar talks with him via video chat.

HAGAR:

Nazeer, tell me what you want.

NAZEER:

I want to ask you something. How long has it been since you had sex?

HAGAR:

Why do you ask this question?

NAZEER:

Just answer me.

HAGAR:

Five months.

NAZEER: *(in a shocked voice)*

Wow! Five months? That's a long time—how are you feeling . . .

HAGAR: *(interrupts him)*

Nazeer, let's be frank. You are not going to send me the

money unless I have video sex with you, right?

NAZEER:

> Don't look at it that way. I just suppose that you must miss being touched. *(Hagar says nothing.)* A beautiful girl like you . . . I know what I would do if I was there with you. I'd come up close to you and take off that scarf. Then I'd run my hands . . .

HAGAR: *(interrupts him)*

> Nazeer, what do you want?

NAZEER:

> I want to see your breasts. Can I?

HAGAR:

> Okay, but when will you send me the money?

NAZEER:

> First thing tomorrow morning.

HAGAR:

> For sure?

NAZEER:

> For sure.

HAGAR:

> Okay.

> > *She walks towards the cake. She looks at Jamal.*

HAGAR:

> Happy birthday, my love. I'm sorry.

> > *She blows out the candle and starts unbuttoning her shirt. The screen goes blank. Lights come back up. We see Hagar on the left side of the stage.*

HAGAR:

> It was your first birthday. I know he didn't touch me, but I felt like I'd been raped. I felt like a whore. I had to do it, so I could run away with you. I thought that would be the worst of it and I could handle the rest. But I was wrong. The road we took was hell.

>> *She scrolls through her photos on her phone. They appear on the backstage screen, showing scenes from her journey from Syria to Turkey. The destruction of the country due to the war is clearly visible from these photos. Some of them show the armed fighters creating road blocks.*

HAGAR:

> It was never easy to see our country destroyed in this way. And it was hard to see strangers in our country starting to take over control, setting up check points and stopping our own people and humiliating them.

>> *She pretends to re-enact a scene at a check point.*

> - Hey, cover yourself woman!
> - I am covered.
> - Cover your face, too, and don't talk. Your voice is a temptation from the devil.

>> *She pretends that someone else is whispering in her ear.*

> -For God's sake shut up, let us go through. Another word and you'll get us all killed.

HAGAR: *(speaking to her son)*

> I looked at your face and at all the passengers and I swallowed my words. I wanted to say lots of things to the armed man. I wanted to ask, who are you? And what are

you doing here? Your accent is weird and you dress weirdly. Your hair, your beards, your gun, and your voices, are all strange. You are not part of us.

I wanted to tell him that this land will swallow you and then spit you out. Many like you have passed through here, but none of them was able to stay. The Hyksos, the Greeks, the Romans, the Tatars, the Turks and the French. All of them left. Our earth, sky, water and blazing spirit spat them out—and you will be the same.

I was looking at these foreigners, and all the destruction around us, I felt such sorrow for us all—even the terrorist holding his gun to our heads. I looked into his eyes and saw an entire life. I saw the brainwashing he went through as a child, about God, religion and life in heaven . . . the virgins in heaven and the tortures of hell. I saw in his eyes the Imam of the mosque telling him that anyone who violates your beliefs is an infidel and should be killed. I saw his mother's eyes waiting for him. I imagined he would be killed so his children would grow up without a father. Then another deluded moron would come along to teach them that killing makes the word of God supreme.

I wanted to tell him that we have learned to love all people. But we cannot love you because you kill our children. So, we can never sympathize with your brutal cause. You and Abouarif and Nazeer and all of you are the same. You are the poor people, not us. You are poor because you live without humanity. You are the monsters, the rabble, the mercenaries. I had a lot to say to this man, but I could not. I had to shut up before he became violent. I covered my face and kept my mouth shut.

- Welcome to Turkey!
- Thank you Abouarif.

- Do you have your money?
- Yes.

He didn't ask me about my dangerous journey. He didn't ask How are you? or How is your baby?

- Do you have the whole lot?
- Yes.
- So, let's go to the hotel.

I could tell you Izmir is a beautiful city. But I wasn't a tourist, I was a refugee and the sights meant nothing to me. We passed buildings, gardens, schools, and factories. In my mind, all I could see was the wreckage of Syria, our ruined homes. I saw blood everywhere, on the walls, on the curbs; body parts hanging on electricity lines. My God, how hard it is to see your country being slowly destroyed day by day, and you are powerless to stop it.

- Give me your passport.
- Why do you want it?
- I need to get a room for you at the hotel.

I gave him my passport, but I didn't want to. I felt like he'd taken my soul and I'd never get it back. The hotel room was filled with women and children.

As if imitating the voice of a woman in the room.

- How long have you been here?
- One week.
- Why haven't you left yet?
- We're waiting for the manager to tell us when the boat's ready to leave.

Her eyes were filled with worry, unable to force what the future held. The children were excited and hopeful, as they imagined parks, toys and schools.

- When are we leaving, Abouarif?
- Just as soon as the bribes are paid.

I didn't understand, but I knew that he wanted to ensure that everything would go well. We were waiting for the moment to get on the boat. We didn't think that the boat would have a restaurant and cabins, but we didn't think that forty of us would get into a rubber dinghy that could barely fit ten.

- But how?
- Don't worry, it's not far and you have life jackets. We'll sail alongside you until you get there.

We left with Abouarif's yacht beside us. The man in control of our dinghy was one of us.

- Are you sure you can drive it?
- Abouarif taught me—yesterday.
- Yesterday?
- It's okay. Abouarif is beside us.

But he wasn't. The boat was getting further away from us.

- Why is he leaving? What is happening?!

We are forty people, mostly women and children, floating in an inflatable rubber dinghy. Everything around us is blue. All of our lives depend on the air trapped in this rubber dinghy. The waves lift us to the sky, as relentless as our fear, and threaten to draw us down to the bottom of the sea.

Did we escape the threat of death under sniper fire only to die in the water? No, no, we won't die. We will live. God is with us. God is watching and God knows. We have done nothing to deserve this!

- What's happening? What is going on?

The man piloting the boat shouts at us to hold on and tells the men to go to one side of the dinghy and the women and children to the other.

In the voice of the pilot.

- The boat is deflating! All who can swim, get in the water!

HAGAR:

God have mercy on us. Help! Hello, anyone! Please help, Abouarif, coast guards! Anyone!

In the voice of a fellow passenger.

- Calm down sister, a ship will come by and help us.

Five hours go by and half the dinghy is in the water and the other half is floating. No one is coming to help. My feet and hands are frozen.

HAGAR: *(talking to someone in the dinghy)*

- Can you please hold my boy? His lips are so dry. I want to give him some water.

In the voice of another passenger.

- Hold on tight everyone! The next wave will be a big one.

I tried to take my baby back but the wave moved faster than I could. I saw nothing but water until the wave subsided. The dinghy had flipped over and everyone was scattered on the sea.

- Where is the girl that held my boy? Where is my son?
- *(in the voice of the girl)* I don't know, when the wave hit us he slipped out of my hands!
- *(shouting)* Please, did anyone see my baby? Anyone?! For

God's sake, please look for my boy.

I swam for three hours but my boy was gone, my boy was gone!

We hear the sound of a ship.

- Get aboard!
- No, I won't get on the ship. My son lost me here and he will find me here. My Dad taught me, if I was lost, to stay in one place until he finds me. You go. I will wait until he comes. He will come. He will never leave me. I have no one else left, just my son and God. I know that they won't leave me alone. They won't, will they? Will they? Answer me!

She passes out. There is a pause for a few seconds and then she gets up.

- Where are we? Izmir? Why did you bring us back to Izmir?

In the voice of a fellow passenger.

- The Turkish coastguards brought us back. We'll keep trying, don't give up hope we will reach Greece.
- I don't want to go to Greece. I just want my son. We will go back to Syria.

- Your son . . . he drowned. I'm so sorry.

- No, no, he didn't! He didn't. Take me to where he lost me. Don't leave him sleeping alone in the water. Please, he will get cold. My son! Oh, my son! Oh!

She turns the crib around and we see it in a shape of a tombstone.

May God be with you. From now on, the sea is your crib and

the waves are your swing. Today is your second birthday.
No one is invited. Like last year and like every year, I will
blow out your candles alone.

She blows out the candles and the stage goes black.

THE END

—

Editorial assistance for "Hagar" was provided by Michael J Tilleard
and Joanna Blundell.

poetry.

SUSANA CHALUT

⟶⟳

The Song of the Lark—Sixteen Poems

Openness

big skies with no endings
shadows that extend over rolling hills
trees talking the language of movement
lonely men walking through traffic
total openness and the acceptance of vulnerability
as a human condition

Apertura

grandes cielos sin fin
sombras que se extienden sobre las lomas
árboles que hablan el lenguaje del movimiento
apertura total y la aceptación de la vulnerabilidad
como condición humana

Adede

Adede sweeps the 3rd floor
of the City Centre mall
she elegantly takes the dust pan
changes the garbage bags
with considerable care
while she hums
a song from her homeland
that makes the mango grow faster

Maria

aromas are the spices
in Maria's kitchen
Maria did not read or write
but she baked long-lasting memories
                              colours
                              and aromas
that took you to other lands
where stories were written
in flavours and strategic portions

Virginia

You cannot find peace by avoiding life

—V Woolf

I travel with the fishes and tides
I am a water traveler carried away by
the oceans
rhythmical waves brought me to these shores
silence and microscopic worlds surround me
I speak the language of the salt
the drowned ones and the seashells
the birds and the wind bring me news
of dry places that I will never visit
where the hearts of men and women
age differently
where love moves apologetically
where caresses cannot find lovers

Process

these words are taking a different path
I take them carefully
and with the wisdom of the one who
does not fear to enter into the night
as a blind and lonely soul

Proceso

estas palabras están tomando un rumbo diferente
yo las abrazo cuidadosamente
y con la sabiduría del que no teme entrar en la noche
ciego y soliario

Polaroid

the clouds are moving west
graciously
leaving behind a flock of snapshots
fragments of ideas
dying images
a broken polaroid
of fragile recollections

Victoria Promenade

there are 110 steps on the stairs to Victoria Promenade
I counted each of them the night we met
at step 45 you softly touched my hand
we talked about the last concert of the
Tragically Hip and how unfair life was
at step 58 a gentle breeze refreshed
the hot Edmonton summer evening
reminding us of childhood memories
and the unknown to come

Back Alley at 116 Street

the racket of the shopping cart
collecting empty dreams
pigeons hanging on electrical cables
like musical notes of rhythmical feathers
loud trucks delivering dust and wind
potholes growing stress and frustrations
an abandoned and dirty sweater
wet and medium-size

The nature of the gatekeeper

the door opens and closes
letting in memories, aromas,
and old readings
I become the sorter
I pick and hide behind each of them
who am I to judge the blank page?

La naturaleza del guardián

la puerta se abre y cierra
dejando entrar memorias, aromas
y viejas lecturas
me vuelvo el clasificador
elijo y me escondo detrás de estos recuerdos
quien soy yo para juzgar la página en blanco?

Intento

when the night comes
I will remember you
conquering all the corners of this old house
everything will stop to transform into your shadow
I will let the hidden memories flood the spaces
of our shared silences
and love will replace solitude
light will replace darkness
caresses will replace emptiness
and for a fraction of a moment
we will feel young and hopeful again
young and hopeful, my love, again

Warmth and Honey

your lips are softly touching mine
timidly and hesitantly first
they remind me of all rivers
and ocean tides
and the wetness of spring rains
motionless instants of peace and sadness together

my lips dancing an ancient choreography
of tensions and impulses
no words fill these mouths now
just warmth and honey

Old Men

I love old men
I love the geography and wrinkles of their hands
the pipes and the yellow-paged newspapers
the playful hairs on their eyebrows
the unbearable fragility of their eyes
eyes of the ones who knew love once
but lost the course because of a misstep

I love old men
I love how they slowly pick their words
to say truth or future
how they walk the aisles of the museums
and churches
contemplating colours and forgotten objects
how they make love
without hurrying
and as if they are denying death

Flexibility

thoughts extending to others
moving and shaping into birds signing
unfamiliar songs
eyes navigating lines of a stanza
the poem written and erased
endlessly

Flexibilidad

pensamientos que se extienden a los otros
moviéndose y transformándose en pájaros que cantan
canciones desconocidas
ojos navegando las líneas de una estanza
el poema escrito y borrado
una y mil veces

Sol

> *En el horizonte de mi mente se ha escondido el sol.*
>
> —los Jaivas

on the horizon of my mind
the sun has set
and I sit here waiting
for a sign
birds fly into the silence
and their shadows follow them
trees continue reciting
the song of the water
and planes leave airports
where lovers say
their goodbyes
holding onto the last kiss
en el horizonte de mi mente se ha escondido el sol
on the horizon of my mind
the sun has set

The Name of Things

to write and write the name of things:
to say January instead of hope
or lion instead of abandonment
to create by naming colours, objects, and seasons
a tower of words
striking the page
collapsing over the edges
hanging onto prepositions
falling off the margins
dead and forgotten

to speak the language of small and big
creatures
the language of universal images
where we all are
one word
one poem sung in many tongues
but repeating the same stanza:
to love and be loved
to love and be loved

13 Sounds

everything written is a step closer
to immortality
thought recordings of men
who once loved and their lovers
disappeared down foggy paths
leaving behind a stela of words
and pain
rusty collectables that became
good or bad poems to be read in
bars or university classrooms
poetry is my homeland, the poet said,
and the lark sang the 13 sounds of its song

Author's Note

I think of myself as a collector. I collect words and images as well as experiences. I came to Canada eighteen years ago and I became busy with life like any other immigrant. Canada gave me two children, a husband, a career, and a home to take care of. I decided to throw myself into this adventure with all my passion. I did not write for fourteen years. However, during these years, I dedicated myself to collecting the ideas which have become my poetry now. The process was slow and it is still happening. My method in approaching poetry was exactly the same in English and Spanish. Reading allows me to understand poetry in different perspectives. I am constantly reading T S Elliot's and Robert Frost's poems (among others) which are the mantras that help me continue with this challenge. Music has also been an ally when I need to start a text. Miles Davis and John Coltrane always take me to the place where I am ready to face the blank page peacefully. I do not translate unless it is totally necessary. I prefer to insert a Spanish word instead. I always keep my mind open and I humbly accept editing help from everybody in my family and around me. I have become very needy grammatically speaking. The search for my English voice is an ongoing process and, like life, it requires hard work and lots of editing.

LUCIANA ERREGUE-SACCHI

⌒

Twelve Poems

*The Embroiderer from Harrods, Argentina (My Grand-
mother Juana Laboureau)*

Here I am, and also the first word,
Délicate.
Never saw her as delicate, delicate.
Only the filaments she teased from the wrought-iron gates
in Parc Monceau,
weaving the barbed wire hovering over the Pampas,
nightly lashings of celadon and gold,
satin stitch,
backstitch,
cross stitch,
split stitch.
Broke the ghostliest linen sent from Buenos Aires
all the way to
Brandsen, where she lived.
Before I return the remaining thread
to Paris,
her final suture, I spell "Long threads you must avoid, they tangle
like lazy thoughts!
Stitch two moments with words, then pull
hard."

La Bordadora de Harrods, Argentina *(Mi Abuela Juana Laboureau)*

Acá estoy, y conmigo la primer palabra,
Délicate.
Nunca la ví ser delicada, delicados.
Eran sólo los filamentos que extrajo de la reja de hierro forjado
en Parc Monceau
con los que unió los alambres de púa que sobrevuelan sobre la
    Pampa
nocturnos latigazos de verde nilo y dorado en
punto satin,
punto atrás,
punto cruz,
punto yerba.
Rompían el lino más fantasmal enviado desde Buenos Aires
hasta la misma ciudad de
Brandsen, donde ella vivía.
Debo retornar el hilo restante
a París, pero antes
deletreo su última sutura
"Tienes que evitar las hebras largas,
se enredan como las ideas de los haraganes!
Borda dos momentos con palabras, y tira
fuerte."

Corset

Lend me your corset
and from the inside
I will paint flora
from Argentina.
Blue jacarandas,
Ceibos that sprout in me like aortas,
forgotten tangoes.
All of my fears

made out of *gesso*.
Like a blank canvas,
you decorated it from the outside
with hammer, sickle,
a starry torso,
your stillborn baby,
and your blue aura.

I want your corset
to embed my trauma,
like Guadalupe Virgin's *Tilmatli*,
so I don't have to
leave my life here,
to gasp for air
or disappear.

Melancholy of the Ancient World

To this day I detest apples.
Blame Snow White and God.
My neighbour's walled garden
paraiso of agapanthus
and *maracuyá,*
was Eden instead.

On that Arcadian January,
nineteen seventy-three,
three Wise Men
broke free from my Christmas
wrapping paper
on their golden camels
right above my house.
I was looking at the
clouds, by then, the sea,
while God,
armless, nude, female,
roamed next door,
in Eden, Brandsen,
Argentina.

Thanks to
Greek artists, and Big Pharma,
divinity appeared
as advertised.

God was,
is,
a miniature.
That Venus of Milo

with the stoic countenance
of classical androgyny
courtesy of synthetic hormones,
immobile, legless,
on a pedestal that read Eugynon.

Of Mothers and Madonnas

What if I told you that *this* mother has no shroud
like the emperor no clothes,
that the Madonna's blue veil is only hers and hers alone,
like hers are all *this* mother's sins.
That *this* mother manufactured sainthood
courtesy of early years of handholding
alongside *her* own mother,
blurred motherhood in training,
walking the small-town centre
to the grocer, the boutique, the bank.

What if I told you doubt never left *her*, so she left.

For the time being, *she* wants you to remember
her ablations, abortions, other men. Oh, the men!
And how
without a second of a doubt this time,
she retrieves at will and then compares
and contrasts
all the Madonnas she ever prayed to—
the one of the Rocks being her favourite,
the Madonna of the Rags in Rotterdam,
one last Madonna, or perhaps her first,
she can remember only
through her grandmother's smoke,
Señora Santa Ana,
hearing once again
Porque llora el niño por una manzana que se le ha perdido,
tú ven a mi casa yo te daré dos, una para el niño y otra para vos.

The Tree of Oblivion

*En mi pago hay un arbol/que del olvido se llama/donde
van a consolarse vidalita/ los muribundos del alma (El
arbol del olvido, milonga)*

The only
unsafe tree
is the tree of oblivion . . .
struck safely down the middle,
on River Lot 7.

Neither Manitoba, nor maple,
this tree willfully remembers
following Laurent Garneau,
son of a trader and
an Ojibwa woman.

Taking in our smoky thoughts,
construction sites
and exhaust fumes,
the Garneau tree greyed, decoding
a taxonomy of uprooting.

Openly
oozing ghost stories
down the middle of its scar,
we drew heads of boys and branches
too long ago, lost to ashes,
drowned in the black milk we drank.

For we paired
into oblivion
no Garneau, no Manitoba,

no maple,
no blooms,
no branches,
not even ghosts,
no *nosotros*.

Game of Thorns

> *Only the flower is born, not the thorn.*
>
> —Giambattista Marino

"Read me this poem about the rose,"
passing me your phone.
La Princesa está triste . . . I begin.
"It is too fast, read it slowly.
Ah . . . her strawberry mouth." You inhale
as I remember
Only the flower is born, not the thorn,
offering you the same white rose
Martí offered in June and January,
simultaneously translating,
reciting, quoting.
In short,
the way we always do
as you recall discussing
Borges and his rose
with a young girl who never read him.
Me neither, by the way,
but never mind,
you assume I did, inhaling,
seeing the rose for the first time.
When I
reassure you
La Princesa is a young girl,
her strawberry mouth all yours, eternally,
because
only the flower is born
not the thorn,
torn, always, flower, not
Boca de fresa.

And you play
with me, with her,
with Borges,
with Martí,
inhaling
strawberry mouth
strawberry mouth
strawberry mouth.

Promises Do Not Hold in the Mountains

Promises do not hold
in the mountains.
Blame the light packed snow
of avalanches,
the compressive,
tensile, sheer
strength of individual
snow layers within snow covers,
diverging substantially in space
and time.

As I leave Banff,
lightly packed promises,
years of ancient and new snow
remain, rolling over me
until their sheer weight
compounds in years.

Until the *Glacier Trail* becomes
a tensile trail of promises,
of snow,
of tears,
of ice.
A fresh path for you
to commune with your ghosts
or a new avalanche
or both.

Back in Edmonton,
they are forecasting
between two and twenty centimeters
of fresh snow.
New promises
remaining on the ground until April at least—
it is the prairie, after all.

Shoes

In my next life,
I will reincarnate
as Michelangelo's
fabled marble slab
and write in perfect English
about the placid life
of frogs in the pond, for example,
or Grecian urns.
Why waste time with angst?
you may ask, gentle reader . . .

Let's not get carried away by the confessional.

The thing is, I still own the body I am in
and it weighs
a lot more than
my 62 kilos.
After 25 years in Canada,
yes, I am metric.
The other thing is, I need to outsource
mi otro idioma,
mi madrelingua,
mi otro yo,
es decir.
My distances,
dislocations,
interruptions.
Life's loose ends.
Just for a little while,
while I take a break
from immigrating,

from the "And so where are you from?"
#Instadifferent #instaassumption #instabasta
and any other hashtag

on your media-friendly feed.
So, bear with me.
And since we are here,
would you please
help me do some heavy lifting?
Lighten my load,
wearing my accented shoes
for as long as you wish.

Ulmus

Branched—
we depart, we contort,
we distort our history.
Our choice was really our exile,
cornering as we left our slap-dash spur-of-the-moment mistakes
towards the boxwood hedge. Hedged,
betting we would finally see what this life was all about.
Here we regroup, we reassess, we reassure each other because
it rains harder under the elm trees
and our words refuse to huddle beneath the high tunnel.

On a side note, why did we desert those other elms?

Enough of memories, pain demands
remaining stubbornly in the present, pretending it's not here.
Let's acknowledge our ghost trees and move on because
this is a one off and from here on it is smooth sailing,
although we can see in between the knotted trunks
just how the imagined landscape really feels.

We both agree to divide and conquer
this wasteland
while we wait
for the storm to pass,
while we waste away
our best resources, our memories,
our years of enduring by accident.
Yes, there,
I said it.

On a side note, why did we do it?

Our words refuse to huddle
under the elm trees,

consistently dripping
countries, addresses, winter coats,
old cd's, fishing gear, craft materials,
Christmas decor, photo albums,
school diplomas, and a glue gun,
leaf litter, useless foliage.

On a side note, why,
no matter how sturdy,
our branches will not hold—
withering like their tall
ancestor trees, full of anger
before the ruins of Troy?

Shrove Tuesday

I am a fifty-year old woman dressing dolls from the 1930s. I pull out drawers containing contorted bodies, naked plastic, tin-metal and sometimes human hair cocooned in gauze-covered collars. Then I enter the number they have in the back of their necks on a database and search for the accompanying objects, clothing and dress them up accordingly. Some dolls are made in Germany, the ones with the natural hair, and I get to experience how the hair of Margarethe would have looked in 1930s Dresden, for example. I cannot find Shulamith's ashen hair just yet, although I managed to dress an "Oriental doll" in his bright orange kimono, as if he had escaped from the opera Mikado or a Cole Porter song . . . After lunch, the conservation kids invite us all to partake in a pancake extravaganza to celebrate Shrove Tuesday. Eating the juicy fruit in the kitchen of this mausoleum, the dolls from the 1930s flash before my eyes, in all their naked plastic, celluloid glory, so I finish eating quickly and get up to rinse my maple syrup-soaked dishes, to shake off the weird feeling that I, too, have a number in my back, that I am naked, in front of all these young conservators, a contorted body out of a drawer, ready to be classified in a database of an empty museum, all natural hair, no plastic, because plastic is so not 2018.

A Ghazal

Alongside the crisscrossing patterns of our discontent
Dye me in the blue hue of your regrets

Red blips I touch, red lip-kissed last letters red lies
Merging my red Latina blood with the hue of your regrets

I dream of gentle verses, vanishing roses, aspen leaves, gliding
    oars,
No need to sleep under the verdant hue of your regrets . . .

Volcanic rocks know nothing about exiles, miasmas, a poem, a
    mistake,
Ovidian ghosts trapped, like moths, inside the amber hue of your
    regrets . . .

I must thank you for the gift of your now dismantled Library of
    Babel
Yes, now, embedding myself in the yellowed hue of your regrets . . .

My Apple

My apple, want a bite?
Let it roll down my
hilly, olive lawn.
Who knows where it may stop?

With all the other
fallen ones . . . visibly rotten.
Otherwise,
in Saxony, 1508,
Lucas Cranach's
Eve,
stands, unrepentant—
Venus Pudica—
shame separating her
from her Luther-loving Adam
already absolved from sin.

By the tree,
yes, that one
you see in my selfie—
Edmonton, 2017—
who knows where it may stop?

Between two realms,
warped wood boards
where warped old Cranach
still plays God,
his Adam pointing right,
frenzied gaze trespassing
the bark of the apple tree, to reach for Her.

And her breasts, already rotten, hilly, olive
on the other side of knowledge,
wary of the snake

who coolly eyes their fate
as that of others
that will bite
from yet another apple.
Who knows where it may stop?

Our state cannot be severed; we are one.
My apple, want a bite?

Author's Note

When I was asked to write on the concept of the Writer as Artist, at first I thought *How am I going to bridge the distance between the general and the personal?* Then I remembered what Caterina Edwards and Jean Crozier taught me in their memoir workshop, "Write what you know." I know of art; I am an art historian and think mostly through images. My mentor and friend, the writer Jaspreet Singh, once asked me after a good six months of writing and reading poetry intensely and incessantly, "So, do you see yourself as a writer now?" To which I replied, "Not at all." His come-back was swift and strangely reassuring: "This is great, because the day you start believing you are a writer, that is when your writing begins to suffer."

So, I write what I know (Art history, Argentinian history, my life in the Pampas during the dictatorship of the 1970s, womanhood, motherhood, and immigration to Canada), yet I still believe I am not a writer, but a reader, and a spectator of art. My memory recalls Marcel Duchamp and his work *Fountain* (1917), an upside-down urinal that he purchased from a sanitary-ware supplier and submitted under the pseudonym "R Mutt" to the show of the newly established Society of Independent Artists in New York. This simple act ushered in Modern Art, all the newest art forms that make us question *How is this art? My child could do that!* (no, he or she can't, by the way) and its ethos: it is art because the artist says it is.

Borrowing from Duchamp, my poems are part of Canadian

Literature, because I say they are. We multilingual immigrants who write, must consider ourselves part of the Canadian literary canon, as a courageous act of agency that transcends the official bilingual model, because we are a Multicultural-Multilingual nation. As I wrote in my poem "My Apple": *Who knows where it may end?* Because doubt and uncertainty offer opportunities for artistic discovery and in art we may find strength.

—

"The Embroiderer from Harrods, Argentina (My Grandmother Juana Laboureau)" was published in Spanish in the Mexican online literary magazine, *La Rabia del Axolotl*, 2017. I wrote this poem thinking of my maternal grandmother's French ancestry as I was landing in Paris last June, the month of her birthday. Despite the very feminine occupation of embroiderer, she was anything but, watching boxing matches on TV and smoking until two in the morning, arguing constantly about politics and wishing she had been born a man.

"Corset" was published in the *Stroll of Poets Anthology 2017*. The poem is inspired by Spanish nursery rhymes that my paternal grandmother recited to me at bedtime, and the poems of Uruguayan poet Juana de Ibarbourou. The line *all of my fears* is after Frida Kahlo's plaster painted corsets. The *Ceibo* tree is very resistant to both ice and fire and a symbol of courage and strength in the face of adversity.

"Melancholy of the Ancient World." When I was four, the Venus of Milo stared at me from the shelf at my great aunt's house and I never forgot about it. Because she was a midwife, she received advertising materials like the miniature image of the Venus of Milo that inspired this poem, from world-renowned contraceptive manufacturer Eugynon. Drug representatives would go door to door to medical professionals living in the remote Pampas. Lilí was a formidable septuagenarian with the chicest blonde *chignon*, silk shift midi dresses in floral prints, grey suede stacked heel pumps, and Peggy Guggenheim spectacles. Until age eighty, traveling by horse drawn buggies to remote farms, rain or shine, she delivered babies with the elegant precision of a watchmaker.

"Shoes" is a direct response to an interview I read in the *The Malahat Review*, where a modernist, white, male poet was critical of confessional poetry. The more I thought about it, the more I realized it reflected his academic training and erudition. It also demonstrated the privileged position and blindness of those who do not see or have to perform the emotional labour that accompanies literary production and the carving of a literary career as a multilingual female Latin American-Canadian writer. My response was instant. I wanted to write about how it felt to be on this side of the spectrum; it is a reflection, a rant, a reckoning, and ultimately a very direct invitation to put ourselves in other people's shoes because it is 2018, in Canada.

Elm trees have been associated in classical literature either with the tree of Paradise or to death as an omen. In my neighbourhood of Belgravia, and also in Garneau some streets are home to high tunnels of elms. The image of hard rain under a canopy of elms came to me last spring as I was walking to Whyte Ave.

NERMEEN YOUSSEF

— ⊃

Extinct

Mama
this is my last letter to you
I know you are confused
that my words are carved
on a block of ice this time
I have no choice
I own nothing

glaciers   have   room   for   all
                    yet
colours choose to escape
here, they left Ice Blue behind
the poor colour shivers in the day
hides between crevices of white
when it is dark it wails
lulled only by the majesty of night

I know you only trust your eyes
to believe this
but yours will never meet Ice Blue
you will never visit me
I am weary of waiting and
wise enough not to expect reunion

nobody noticed when I was stabbed
they were diligently collecting snowflakes
building higher mountains
in hopes of finally seeing the sun
I chose to be silent
nobody believes drifters

a stray river slices

through ice

pulsates

carries memories of

home
carries memories of you

today marks my six thousandth year
and my only friend is a

limping magpie
he still hasn't stopped smoking his pipe
no matter how many times death called on his lungs
deep down I know that this bird will outlive me
it will outlive all of us

not all stabs are sinister
the icicle brought us life
Fresh Red
embracing
Ice Blue

after Red left
I blended in seamlessly
chalk white   flat line
prerequisites for sanity on the glacier

I never asked the magpie about his

limp
he never asked why an icicle stuck
out of my chest
we talked about lands he limped on
and those my heart loved back
when it could
distinguish

Mama,
the snow globe is devious
the inside is nothing you could have imagined
it is nothing you told me it would be
I am not blaming you

the magpie is silent
it tried to escape with the rest of the colours
hit its head in the glass
fell back onto the frigid ground
it tried again
each try
a stitch pulled his wings tighter together
each try
tired wings grew heavier with resentment

wings sewn shut
featherless
no flying back

to this day
they do not know the name
you gave me

their language is nods
I practiced
up
then
down
then up and down again
smile optional
nervousness preferred
I was wrong

they spoke to my curls
I heard them
many times
a phantom I stood between them
Why them and not me?
I went to the river to complain to you
their permanent reflection mocked me
you were silent
I threatened them with guillotines
they laughed louder
my rage echoed   it scared me
not them
their springs rusty and frozen
familiar with threats
now too weak to echo

Mama,
the stories of exile are eerily similar
even accompanied by the same music
the *A minor* of impending doom
after a few hundred years
there are no stories
no surprises
flat line

their mountain is high
so high
it blocks the sun

sitting on the edge of this floating continent
hoping to spot empathy in the distance
maybe even a wandering colour
do I truly remember colour?
are there shades between Chalk White and Ice Blue?

Mama,
I trained myself to pull
both edges of my mouth sideways
they told me I have healed

Mama,
I decided
today will be my last on the Glacier
I will pack my curls and leave
hoping they will find
company with yours

I'm coming home

journalism.

TAZEEN HASAN

⟋⟍⟍⟍⟍⟍⟍⟍⟍⟍⟍⟍⟍⟍⟍⟍⟍⟍⟍⟍⟍⟍⟍⟍⟍⟍⟍⟍⟍⟍⟍⟍⟍⟍⟍⟍

The Namesake: Values That Change

Mira Nair's touching cross-cultural saga, *The Namesake*, is a narrative of a Bengali family's migration to the United States, and its cultural transformation through the course of two generations. The parent-child story is about the values that change across geographies, cultures, and generations and the values that stay intact throughout.

The film, based on a novel by the Pulitzer Prize-winning author Jhumpa Lahiri captures the emotional outcomes of human migration, particularly the loss of old and integration of new identities, and the consequential generational gaps between migrant parents and their first-born American offspring. These themes are not specifically Indian and so the film has been able to reach out across cultural, racial, and religious boundaries to resonate with immigrant experiences of varying backgrounds.

Nair has a knack for exposing brutal social and cultural realities with a remarkably high degree of subtlety. After several true-to-life documentaries, she demonstrated her exceptional mastery of cinematic syntax with her first feature film, *Salaam Bombay*, capturing the miserable life of street children using a cast of actual street children. The film won 23 international awards and was nominated for Best Foreign Language Film at the Academy Awards. Her later films also met with critical acclaim and became major box office successes. Lahiri, Nair, and Sooni Taraporivala (the scriptwriter), all have Indian-American backgrounds so they have brought their own experiences to authentically deal with Indian subjects in *The Namesake*. The result is an emotionally resonant family portrait that entertains with subtle charms.

Ashoke Ganguli (Irfan Khan), a Bengali fiber-optic researcher in the United States, had miraculously survived an almost fatal train accident in his teenage years in India, only because instead of sleeping, he had been reading "The Overcoat" by Nikolai Gogol. Before the train wreck, a fellow passenger persuaded him to move abroad, "Pack a pillow and blanket. See the world." This inspires Ashoke to leave India and pursue the American dream. He marries Ashima (Tabu), and Gogol (Kal Penn) and Sonia (Sahira Nair) are born. Gogol's name by itself carries a strong emotional anchor for Ashoke that the America-born Gogol can't relate to, like his other parental Bengali mores. The story progresses smoothly through the family routine and social life, the intermittent long-distance calls announcing the death of close relatives, as well as the frequent trips to India. Lahiri meticulously paints the story through a layered perspective using multiple protagonists, thus evoking empathy for each one of them. Thoughtful performances combined with elaborate lighting and careful sound design enhance the alternating emotions of delight, sadness, fear, and humour.

Presumably, the novel reflects Lahiri's own life. Born Nilinjana, she changed her first name exactly like Gogol did in the novel. Like Ashima, Lahiri's mother also wanted her children to grow up knowing their Bengali heritage, and like the Gangulis, her family often visited relatives in Calcutta. Her Bengali background, coupled with her upbringing in the States gave her the insight to develop Gogol's persona with deep credibility.

The Ganguli parents find it hard to leave their past behind but are prepared to sacrifice everything for their future in the new land. Right from Gogol's birth, Ashima is overly sensitive about his upbringing in what is to her a strange society, but Ashoke calms her apprehensions, saying, "It is the land of infinite opportunities." No matter how much the people of the developing world bash America for the ongoing geopolitical chaos in the world, individuals continue to yearn to move to the western hemisphere and especially to the United States. However, once the migrant families have settled down, they confront an inevitable identity crisis. As their first-born American children approach their teenage years, the parents begin to sense a cultural divide and a communication gap with their offspring. Like many migrant parents in the 1970s and 1980s, the Gangulis couldn't envision these identity issues until they suddenly saw them in their teenagers. As Ashima sadly laments, "I feel I have given birth to strangers."

Cultural identity is a complex phenomenon emanating from family values, ethnicity, religion, generation, nationality, and the distinct social group in which one finds affinity and belonging. It is fluid in nature and often undergoes a metamorphosis with the fusion of different cultures. This change can lead to strong societal integration but can also lead to a diminishing of less powerful diaspora cultures. The Gangulis identified themselves as Hindu Bengalis from India. Back home in Calcutta, they had strong ethnic and religious traditions, in contrast with the less patriarchal American culture. Overwhelmed by their sense of alienation and nostalgia, the Gangulis confine their socializing to Bengali families, sharing their happy and sad moments and celebrating their festivals. Gogol, however, finds it hypocritical to join the Indian Association at the University, "an organization that willingly celebrates occasions his parents forced him [to attend]."

Penn skillfully manages the complex role of a man straddling two cultures. His facial expressions are etched with the conflict roiling inside him. Gogol's hybrid persona progresses from that of a child experiencing two contrasting ways of life to that of a mature adult totally submissive to the American lifestyle. As a child, he had regularly overheard midnight long-distance telephone calls announcing the deaths of close relatives in India and seen his parent's shocked reactions. Yet, unlike his parents, he never thinks of India as a "Desh" (Motherland). And while his mother "weeps with relief" on landing in India, he dreads the thought of spending another vacation in a place where he finds nothing to do. During his university years, he gradually drifts away from his family. Later, while staying with his white girlfriend Maxine (Jacinda Barrett), he cannot help comparing the unsophisticated lifestyle of his family with the refined manners of the Ratliffs (Maxine's family) in matters of food, hospitality, sex, romance, and social lives.

The inner conflict of a generation sandwiched between two cultures, tagged in the novel as American Born Confused Desi (ABCD), is portrayed exquisitely through the psyche of Moushumi (Zulekha Robinson), a highly educated daughter of Bengali parents, who unwillingly follows her parent's advice from her childhood while loathing Indian values. She escapes to Paris and adopts an uninhibited attitude towards sex, for example, "allowed the men to buy her drinks, dinner and later to take her in taxis to their apartments." Yet when her American fiancée criticizes India after a trip to Calcutta, she throws her engagement ring in a trash can. "For it was one thing for her [. . .] to reject her family heritage, another to hear it from him." Similarly, Gogol is more than a little upset when an old lady ridicules him at a party by asking stereotypical questions about India. Conversely, he is flattered when his girlfriends show respect for India.

As a recent immigrant, having observed the immigrant experiences of my extended family closely since the mid-1990s, I believe things have changed considerably since the novel was written. With a massive influx of immigrants both in the United States and Canada, diaspora communities are much more resilient now and are better prepared to cope with the identity dilemma. Moreover, in the digital era, they have access to effective diasporic media which strengthen them and simultaneously keep them well-connected to their home country and culture.

However, there is still a host of real-life issues that constantly haunt immigrant parents, for example, sex-before-marriage and the LGBT culture. These conventions of North American society remain a taboo in certain conservative diasporic communities. In the novel, when Gogol's relationship with Ruth is exposed, the Gangulis become concerned. It only makes things worse when Gogol responds that "marriage is the last thing" on his mind. Similarly, in a film scene, Ashima asks her colleague about Gogol's girlfriend, "What kind of a girl is called Max?" and her friend replies, "Maybe it's a boy." I can well imagine how shocking this could be for a South Asian mother to discover that her son is gay. Later, before Maxine visits his parents, Gogol counsels her, "No kissing, no holding hands."

Furthermore, most immigrant parents try to convince their offspring to marry inside their own communities as a surefire way to preserve cultural heritage. Before Gogol departs for Yale University, his aunt prudently advises him not to desist from having fun with others, but, to "Marry a Bengali." Later, after gradually accepting Gogol's rejection of Indian values, Ashima arranges for him to meet Moushumi. They both enjoy their first meeting as some sort of an arranged date to please their parents. One significant outcome of this meeting is that it coaxes him to resort to Bengali in his conversation with a cabbie, bluntly signaling his return to the parental fold.

It is my very personal observation that immigrant children pick up the language of the dominant host culture almost instantly, while their parents continue to struggle with language skills for a long time, and this further amplifies the communication gap between the generations. Diaspora communities often overlook the fact that their mother tongue plays a key role in preserving parental identity as a link between the generations and cultural heritage. As the usage of the mother tongue diminishes, oral traditions also fade away. The Gangulis arranged Bengali classes for their children but weekend classes don't help much in the English-speaking world all around.

Not all of the Gangulis' efforts are wasted in the long run. At a certain phase in his life, Gogol finally returns to his parental values and understands the emotional baggage his parents brought along with them from India. The story of the Gangulis is a message that during the process of integration, the salient features of the parental

culture finally survive and ultimately new generations learn to bal-
ance their old and new identities. The Ivy League graduate Gogol
shaves his head voluntarily and scatters the ashes of his father in the
Ganges to signify his adoption of Bengali customs.

The Namesake reveals many migrant issues subtly through the
Gangulis but one aspect of immigration that the film couldn't grasp
is the inverted impact of cultural transformation. It is historically
evident that during the assimilation process, the diaspora not only
struggles to retain their specific cultural traits but simultaneously
influences those in their adopted lands. The Indian Diaspora in the
United States is perhaps one of the successful examples of this integration: the Gangulis are a part of the North American academic
elite, serving and studying in top American Universities. Similarly,
other immigrant communities have also visibly impacted American
life, for example in the changing American attitudes towards food
(Sushi, Biryani, kabobs, Chinese, and Mexican food). But in the film,
which closely follows the novel, none of the Americans seem to learn
anything from the Gangulis.

Cinematographer Frederick Elmes collaborated closely with Nair
to capture the contrasting city lives of Manhattan and Calcutta from
appealing angles. Together they weave a rich tapestry of Indian
scenery through documentary-style shots of the middle-class neigh-
borhoods of Calcutta, an exciting tram trip through packed streets,
and gorgeous shots of the 150-year-old historic Howrah railway
station swarming with people. Yet, the Ganguli children are not
impressed by the colourful Indian culture and by layers of its intricate
history until a view of the Taj Mahal mesmerizes them, and Gogol
finally decides to become a professional architect. Until this point,
the Ganguli parents have largely failed to evoke in their children a
sense of pride in their parental land. Besides the superb camera work,
the awe and excitement engraved on Penn's face during the shots
showcasing the Taj Mahal evoke an equally unforgettable experience
for the viewers.

The film closely follows Lahiri's story but for some unknown reason, the setting of the film version of the story has been changed from Boston to New York and moved forward a decade. Besides, many sensitive moments are overlooked, for example, Gogol and Maxine's break-up is shown hastily at the funeral gathering but in the novel, Lahiri handles it carefully.

However, Lahiri and Taraporivala do not delve deeply into the characters of Ashoke and Ashima. Ashima's emotions are deeply hidden, at least in the first half of the film; neither she nor the crowd of Indian relatives around her look excited about her moving to America. Although she is portrayed as an educated girl, she has no positive feelings about moving from the crowded poverty-stricken streets of Calcutta to a neighborhood close to Harvard Yard (in the novel) or the film's New York suburb. All she notices is a terrible laundromat across the street in Central Square and small apartments instead of the townhouses with playground-length lawns she had seen earlier on television in India. Ashoke is characterized as a compassionate husband and a cool father. The film closely follows the family life, but the couple hardly has a conflict in their marital life except over a shrunken shirt.

Irfan Khan (Ashoke) and Tabu (Ashima), two of Bollywood's accomplished names who emerged from low budget films, do a marvelous job as usual. They reveal the intricacies of the family relationship through a quiet glance or a shrug without overplaying their roles. Portraying a highly-educated nerd who could never forget the horror of the train wreck, Khan's performance is excellent with his Bengali-accented English and shy gestures. As the main protagonist, Penn's performance is equally matched by his Bollywood counterparts.

There are countless films highlighting immigrant experiences, each with a diverse perspective. However, I believe, the closest story that deals with the interlinked themes of immigrant experience, family bondage, and identity crisis is a Pakistani drama serial, *Bilquis Kaur*. Bilquis Kaur, a Sikh Punjabi-American, elopes from her house to marry a Pakistani in New York. She rules her family like a dictator, enforcing centuries-old Punjabi traditions until her children revolt. In contrast to the highly educated Gangulis, this engaging and realistic serial portrays a working-class family. Character development, as well as the performances, are brilliant, but this low-budget work is far behind *The Namesake* as far as nuance and subtlety are concerned.

Human Migration is as old as mankind. Historical terms such as Exodus, Diaspora, Aaliyah, and Hejira each narrate a unique tale. Migrant families face agonizing challenges in new lands, not the least important of which is to learn how to integrate within a new society without leaving their past behind. *The Namesake* is a comprehensive illustration of this three-decade-long journey compressed into two hours. Generally, universal themes succumb to banal and hackneyed stereotypes, but the film poignantly explores the dilemmas of assimilation and identity crises faced by diaspora communities through a flawless story, arresting performances, and a touching musical composition. Nair tenderly handled Lahiri's realistic tones. No doubt, the film rejuvenates the novel experience and speaks volumes to anyone who has ever felt a push-pull relationship with his or her heritage.

Fighting Stereotypes in Popular Media

It was 2014. I had recently arrived in Canada and during an informal conversation at a seminar, a female immigrant from Mexico praised me for being bold and expressive, and she inquired about my nationality. My response seemed to surprise her. "You look educated," she blurted out. "I had the impression that Pakistani women were not allowed to study." I was offended. "What made you think that Pakistani women were not allowed to study?" I asked politely. "No idea," she replied, simply shrugging her shoulders.

Oriental societies and their cultures have been depicted negatively for centuries, enforcing misleading stereotypes. But after 9/11, this has been narrowed to Muslim and Pakistani societies in the media and political discourse. The media, in the form of news, fiction, non-fiction, film, literary journalism, and talk shows has gone out of its way to cultivate the image of the oppressed Muslim woman. Islam has become synonymous with terrorism, a Muslim man with violence, and a Muslim woman with the oppressed.

A Muslim woman is often portrayed as someone who is forced by her family and society to cover her head and face, is verbally and physically abused in her home, and is not allowed to study, work, or travel freely. The Western world stereotypes Muslim women largely through the lens of two-time Oscar winner Sharmeen Obaid-Chinoy, *The New York Times* Best Seller authors Khalid Hussaini and Azar Nafisi, and the story of Nobel Prize winner Malala Yousufzai.

These writers and film-makers have sketched a certain class and background of Muslim life, largely highlighting extreme attitudes and isolated incidents that have rarely been endorsed by Muslim societies themselves.

Contrary to those who paint the world's 1.7 billion Muslims with a broad brush, I have spent about four decades living and experiencing various Muslim societies. My extensive travels, which include visits to some of the most remote and isolated regions in the Muslim world, as well as urban centres of the Western world, have influenced and shaped my stance as a champion of women's rights. While I have spoken out against misogynistic practices in my own culture, I cannot accept this one-sided, fabricated generalized sketch of Muslim cultures and oppressed Muslim women. I am part of a large group of highly educated women who choose to practice their religion proudly and to cover their heads of their own free will. But we have almost no representation in popular Western media. Once, at the Breden Institute in Edmonton, a counselor told me that there are more women engineers from Pakistan and Iran arriving in Canada as immigrants than any other country. Yet women of these two countries are among the most stereotyped.

The majority of Muslim households desire the highest level of education for their daughters. Even Malala's family desired this, though she was born in a lower middle-class family in a remote and isolated mountainous valley in northern Pakistan. Her family, religion, and culture gave her the confidence to struggle against the extremist and radicalized regime of the Taliban. But in the West, Malala is exploited to create a negative image of the whole country. The Pakistani government and society never endorsed the extreme attitudes of the Taliban, who briefly occupied her home region. Malala's story does not mention millions of Pakistani women who receive higher education, nor the tens of thousands of women working as professionals in every field of life.

It is my position that the rhetoric of the oppressed Muslim woman is a feminist version of the "White Man's Burden" used to justify colonialist attitudes. Us versus them, rational versus irrational, and civilized versus barbarian is not a new rhetoric; it has deep roots in colonization and Eurocentric racism. A couple of examples from the last century illustrate my point: A former American official in the Philippines commented in 1899 that the Filipinos are "children, and child-like," and do not know what is best for them. "By the very fact of our superiority of civilization and our greater capacity for industrial activity, we are bound to exercise over them a profound social influence." And Lord Cromer, British Consul General in Egypt said, "The Egyptians should be persuaded or forced to become civilized by disposing of the veil."

More recently, when France banned the Niqab in 2011, French politicians and policy makers said that they were protecting and promoting gender equality and the dignity of women. And now the European Court of Justice has ruled that an employer can fire an employee on the basis of a dress code, directly targeting the hijab. Furthermore, the province of British Columbia failed to pass a bill preventing restaurants from forcing employees to wear high heels. Female freedom and women's rights are again enforced by legislation. Women are always more prone to oppression largely through poverty, ignorance, corruption, and bad government, including the legacy of colonization.

Edward Said's *Orientalism* attacked this colonial mindset around fifty years ago and created many ripples in the academic world, yet it has brought about almost no change in the Western way of thinking. The agenda of civilizing Muslim cultures and setting a Muslim woman free continues in film, literature, and, sometimes, even in academia. So it warrants repeating that Muslim women who cover their heads are often also doctors, engineers, writers, pilots, college and university professors, athletes, and hold offices as parliamentarians and heads of state. Many of these women are champions of women's rights and deserve to be portrayed in literature and film. Can we expect a documentary on the life of Zunera Ishaq, who stood against the former prime minister of Canada, challenged the sitting government, and succeeded in her constitutional struggle to cover her face during the citizenship oath ceremony? The stories of these practising and forward-thinking Muslim women deserve to have a shot at *The New York Times* Best Seller list and the Academy Awards.

memoir.

MILA PHILIPZIG

———⌒

Running in Munich

In 1988, I moved to Munich, Germany on a two-year scholarship. Prior to this, I had been an exchange student in Japan and Canada, so I was not new to being in an unfamiliar place where I did not know anyone. I was a bit apprehensive and unsure but not dismayed at being alone in a foreign country. I knew that being on a scholarship would provide some structure and routine at the beginning, and with language classes, university courses, and sports clubs or choral groups that I intended to join, I would meet people and eventually have friends. Until then, I had lots of time, no friends, and hardly any money. But I knew something that was cheap, enjoyable, easy to do, and was guaranteed to get me out and about instead of holed up in my room—running.

So, I ran.

Running had always been a big part of how I made myself at home in new places. I ran in expanding concentric circles, first around the block where I lived, then slowly spreading outwards, often passing the same places repeatedly to familiarize myself with street names, the landscape, and landmarks. I took note of metro and bus stations, convenience stores, coin laundries, main streets, parks, monuments and other defining structures. In my head, I mapped their location and distance vis-à-vis my new abode. Running offered a direct and palpable way of orienting myself in a new city in ways not possible in a vehicle. There was a certain intimacy in feeling my feet pound the pavement while I immersed myself in the ordinariness of everyday details like big old doors, ornate woodcarvings, candles on window sills, graffiti, cyclists with groceries, neighbours chatting, children being awkward, funny, and adorable. I basked in all the new words swirling around me as I tried to decipher their meanings: Konditorei, Bäckerei, Öffnungszeiten, Viktualienmarkt, Gasthaus, Buchladen, Sonderangebot, Hugendubel, Augustiner-Keller and so on. I let the words roll off my tongue (surely mispronounced), reveled in the different sounds and ways I had to manage my mouth and lips. I had read somewhere that the language one spoke would determine one's looks as the lip movements and most-used facial muscles could shape a person's face. I wondered if I had the facial configuration to speak German well, or if a two-year stay in Germany would leave a mark on my face.

It was exhilarating to do something familiar and gratifying in strange, new places, and allow myself to be open to anything, even, or especially, getting lost. Living in a new country was all about exploration, wonder, and discovery. With that mindset, getting lost was merely an extension of the jaunt rather than something to be feared. Nowadays, with GPS and apps that provide electronic maps and route planning, I do not get lost as much. Even when I turn into paths or alleyways on impulse from time to time, I do not capture the spontaneity and whimsy from my earlier runs.

I suppose walking to scout my new neighborhood would have worked, too. But running allowed me to cover more ground and walking served a different purpose for me. I walked when I had some mundane task that needed to be done—banking, shopping, buying stamps, or seeking out pay phones that accepted international calls.

Running was intentional and vigorous. Walking was unhurried. I took leisurely detours and sought out parks with comfortable benches to read. Walking was also when I tended to linger in bookshops, museums, grocery stores, and open food markets in city squares. I often wished I could pass the time in cafés, but this was a pleasure not easily attained on my student budget. I also often wished I had a camera. But not only did I lack the money to buy a camera, I was too strapped to continuously buy film and pay to have it developed as well. Back then, I relied on postcards if I wanted to remember certain places.

When I walked in foreign cities, I took on a completely different persona than when I ran. I dressed differently for walking and running—I carefully chose outfits, coordinated matching scarves, carried a bag or two, and often an umbrella. But, in contrast, I did not care if I got soaked while running. And I liked the freedom of being unencumbered by bags and wearing shapeless, comfortable sports clothes (there was no fashionable, colourful, and lightweight running wear, at least that I could afford). Running brought me comfort and confidence. I knew exactly what to wear to run, depending on the weather, time of day, and the distance of my route. When I ran I was strong, fast, and disciplined; I was doing something few others did at that time. Outside of running, I was unsure about the character I wanted to project. I was at an age when I was still swayed by fashion, but Asian models in print and screen were rare in Europe, the clothes were not my size, and the makeup did not match my skin tone. I was also in Germany at a time when catalog brides from Asia were common, while the other Asian women were typically pampered, rich travelers. I wasn't either of these, nor did I want to be perceived as if I were. I wanted to be seen as a scholar. But even in this role, I was insecure about my topic, my abilities, my career options, my fashion choices, and my financial deficiency. Running recalibrated my focus—my self-doubts and uncertainties were temporarily banished and replaced by feelings of fulfillment and competence. Long-distance running helped me to be at peace with my thoughts, my environment, myself, and my choices.

So I ran. A lot.

Almost as a ritual, before each run, I lined up what I needed: 10-Pfennig coins for the pay phones, a wrist watch, keys, band aids, transit pass, water bottle, and maps. I laced up my runners, which had my last name and some emergency phone numbers written on the heels. (I learned this as a street-marching activist back home where we wrote codes and lawyer's numbers on our shoes.) I checked my keys. I put on sunglasses for anonymity, and away I went. Once outside, I always looked back and up to the second-floor windows, where inevitably, an older German woman, half-hidden by lacy white curtains, was peering down at me sternly. She was probably wondering why I ran, as so few women did at that time. Running was not as pervasive then as it is now. Before the 1980s, there were no women's distance races in the Olympics, and it was only in 1984 that the Women's Marathon became an Olympic sport. Before that, women were deemed too weak to run long-distances and were forbidden in official races longer than 800 meters. Many women ran unregistered in marathons anyway and eventually paved the way for women long-distance races to be instituted in international competitions. My regular runs were probably strange to the old woman, perhaps in addition to my being foreign. I shrugged that off, but it still always bothered me a bit—until I got into my rhythm and pace. Once in my private running zone, it didn't bother me that people were watching me.

I was delighted to learn that Germany had an abundance of reliable, detailed neighborhood and district maps. Maps allowed me to run longer, free from having to count city blocks, remembering landmarks, or memorizing twists and turns in my paths. Maps allowed me to venture into more places because I could take the bus or metro one way and run back. Maps opened up numerous running spaces and opportunities. I loved pouring over those maps and planning my routes, full of anticipation for what I would see and discover on each route. Pre-internet, there was no easy access to know what one would encounter in places one had never visited before. And so it was that I ran blindly into Brienner Strasse and into the grandeur and magnitude of Königsplatz.

Königsplatz is an enormous square in Munich, modeled after the Acropolis in Athens. In the middle of the main boulevard, Brienner Strasse, is the Propyläen gateway complete with Doric columns. On each side are two massive, templelike museums. Wide and spacious, the whole square is an elegant mix of concrete, grass, and trees. I was in such awe of this monumental place the first time I stumbled into it that I stopped running and spun around to take in this new discovery. I went up and down the gateway steps and touched the columns, wandered into the museums in search of more information about exhibits, and eventually I planted myself on a bench, soaking in the beauty and immensity of Königsplatz. I could hardly believe where I was. I remembered where I came from—one of six siblings orphaned early, sometimes getting only one meal a day, living in a small apartment, sometimes without water or electricity—and I wondered, how could I be here now, exposed to all this beauty? After a while, still overwhelmed, I started running back slowly, as if speed and exuberance would be disrespectful to this awe and grace I was feeling. On my way home, two people stopped me, pointing to a leaflet I had in my hand—from the Glyptothek, a renowned museum for Greek and Roman sculptures. They were looking for it and asked for directions, but they knew very little English, and even less German. I used my map to show them and made sure to tell them to take the main boulevard, Brienner Strasse. I also tried to tell them that Sundays it cost only one Deutschmark. But with hand gestures and swishing sounds, they indicated they would be on a plane on Sunday. We laughed and went our own ways. I felt elated that someone had asked me for directions and I could direct them to such a wonderful place.

I would often return to Königsplatz, even after I discovered the many other delights of Munich, the parks, gardens, architecture, and cityscape. There were so many things to see, so many impressive running routes. On weekends, there were even cheap train tickets available to explore the countryside and hills beyond Munich. Unfortunately, I never found anyone to run with me. But I didn't care. I was in a runner's paradise and felt safe and happy venturing out on my own.

So, I ran. Further and further.

On a clear Sunday afternoon, my plan was a fifteen to eighteen-kilometer run to Aubinger Lohe, west of the city, then further to the creek in Moosschwaige, and then back home. I figured it would take me about two hours. When I got to the park, I heard children shrieking in the playground before I saw any people. Some strolled leisurely around, some sat on long benches at wooden tables shaded by the large trees of the outdoor beer garden. Everything felt safe and welcoming.

I turned away from the crowd and headed towards the path to the trail beyond, mostly shaded by tall spruce trees, which provided welcome shade from the summer sun. It got quieter the further I got from the beer garden and open meadows. I felt especially strong, running faster than my usual pace. I was a bit preoccupied—my scholarship was coming to an end and I really wanted to stay in Europe.

As the path became muddy, I slowed down. Ahead of me, a man was cycling slowly. He waved me down when he saw me. He turned his bike, blocking my path. "Pasing Bahnhof, Pasing Bahnhof," he said, asking for directions. Ah, I knew exactly where the Pasing train station was. As I unfolded my map to show him, he grabbed me.

After
I adjusted my clothes
quietly, methodically
made sure that I
would look decent
for the long way home

After
I sat there
closed and opened my jaw
gasping
willed myself to
braced myself for
willed myself to
shout

move
rage
cry
I could not see clearly
I could not think
I was soundless
on dank dirt
I just sat there
stunned

After
I stood up
my legs remembered
the way to go
left, right
left, right
on and on
without me thinking
My legs remembered
how to get home

I saw strollers
an outdoor café
trees
blue skies
In me
crazed screaming
vile screaming
bile building
anguish screaming
No one heard
no one came
no sound came
I moved
soundless

invisible

Was my pain, my shredded skin, not exposed
Were fragments of me not laid bare
I felt so feeble
and foul
yet not one
no one
could see me
I went on

A telephone
I had ten-*pfennig* coins
I always made sure
I had my coins
Polizei 1-1-0 *anrufen* 1-1-0
it's even free
but I had no words
foreign land
foreign me
I had no words yet

for this
even in my mother tongue
no words
I walked on
If my anguish was so invisible
undefinable
unutterable
was it real

This was not yet real to me
I didn't know what to think
where could I push off all these
thoughts I needed to take in
filth I needed to absorb

but did not wish to
I walked on
My legs
they went
left, right
left, right
on and on
towards home

I got home
I leaned my head on the door
I did not want to bring this
This
I fumbled with my keys
chest exploding
I did not want to bring this
into my home
tears came

My life now
clearly cleaved
into a before and after

Author's Note

I started travelling in the 1980s. Travel literature then was dominated by European or North American male travellers. The perspectives presented were mostly from men who could afford to travel, and who were venturing into places like Africa and Asia where they could stretch their funds. Most information in those books was not applicable nor useful to me. I was female, from a developing country, and I was travelling alone. At that time, plane and train fares were also more expensive, and internet and cell phones were not ubiquitous. Affordability and access to travel, and what one prepared for and paid attention to, were very different than today. From 1980 to 1994, I managed to study and live in Japan, Canada, USA, Germany, Belgium, and the Netherlands on limited funds. Wherever I was, I still managed to get around and know the cities quite well by running long distance.

ASMA SAYED

⟶

Hawa: The Madwoman in the Market

Hawa Gaandi they called her—Mad Hawa. There are many stories about Hawa. From what people knew, Hawa was Muslim. Hawa—the Arabic equivalent of Eve. A reminder of life in the Garden of Eden. But where was Hawa's garden? Where was her home? Maybe Hawa wasn't her real name, but nobody seemed sure. No one knew who she was or where she came from. All they saw was that Hawa begged for food in the main vegetable market of Upleta, ate and wore whatever kind folks gave her, and slept on the streets.

Even today, after more than three decades, in a place far far away from where I first saw her, Hawa roams my memories at odd hours as she did in the streets of Upleta—when I'm driving, in the middle of the night, while I'm grocery-shopping. What was it about Hawa that her memory still haunts me? That I still call my mother in India from my Canadian home, two decades later, and ask her questions about Hawa? Why do I ask my mother to inquire, to find out if anyone knows anything about her? There are so many questions that still linger in my mind. What led to her madness? Was there nobody to help her? Where did she disappear? What happened to her baby? Was she still alive? If not, who buried her? Where? I want to understand the life of a helpless woman who could not tell her story. Even if she could have, nobody seemed to care. She was a woman without support, government or otherwise, whose life I can only resurrect in my memories—or is it my imagination?

Every summer, I with my mother and my siblings went to Upleta to spend time at my grandparents' place. Upleta is a small town in the Rajkot district in the western province of Gujarat in India. Situated on the banks of Moj river and not too far from the Gir Forest National Park, a wildlife sanctuary known for its Asiatic lions, Upleta has its own charm with many beautifully carved temples and mosques adorning its streets. In those days, that is, in the 1970s, it was predominantly Muslim, with a large proportion of people from my community, the Memons, who speak Kutchi, a Gujarati dialect. Most of us are descendants of the Hindu Lohana community, those who are believed to have converted to Islam sometime in the fifteenth century. While there is much anecdotal history of the community, no significant academic study exists. Today, the Memon community is dispersed across the globe with a sizeable number in India, Pakistan, the United Kingdom, Kenya, Tanzania, and in the Unites States and Canada.

Both my parents were born and raised in Upleta. I too am Upleta-born—in the town's Janana Hospital, or Women's Hospital. It is a tradition in many communities in India that after being married women return to their parents' home to give birth to their first child. Women usually stay from the last week or month of pregnancy, to about three months after the birth of the baby, at which point they return to their husband's or in-laws' house. The birthing itself mostly happens in the local women's hospital, but some also choose to deliver the baby at home. So although my parents lived in Porbander, a town close to Upleta, where my father worked as a professor of English, around the time of my birth my mother went to Upleta. We would continue to return to Upleta every summer for the following twenty-five years, to spend some time with my grandparents.

My visits to Upleta were mostly pleasant. I lived a very care-free life during those four to six weeks of every year—the beautiful summer months of April and May. Markets overflowed with mangoes of all kinds—Kesar, Alphonso, and Langdo. *Nanape*, my grandpa, brought mangoes in large wicker baskets. Kesar mangoes were usually bought unripe; they were arranged on a jute cloth and placed under a bed where they would ripen in the warmth and darkness that the space offered. Every day we checked for ripe mangoes and picked out the ones that were ready to eat.

It was during one of those summer visits that I first saw Hawa. I was eight or nine years old. I accompanied my *nanape* to the Sabji Mandi, Upleta's main vegetable market, to buy mangoes. The market was on a busy street shared by bicycles, scooters, rickshaws, horse carriages, and an occasional car. Cows, dogs, and pigs roamed around the market scavenging for food. Vendors displayed vegetables and fruits—tomatoes, eggplants, capsicums, oranges, and apples—in different vibrantly coloured piles all beautifully laid out to entice customers, and they would call out, "Tomatoes fifty paise a kilo, potatoes one rupee a kilo . . . "

Amidst this chaos, I spotted her. I remember a shopkeeper giving her a mango. Today, in my memory, I see her roaming around in worn-out and dirty clothes. She looked like an old woman to me. But when I got home and asked my *nanima*, my grandmother, she said Hawa was probably in her thirties. As she wandered around the vegetable market, one vendor would give her a carrot, another an apple, someone else a ripe black banana that was beyond saleable. I recollect the way she dragged her limping body through the market. As she hobbled, a group of little boys chased after her. She began to run. Then she paused and screamed, "Go away, go away!" The more restless she became, the more fun the boys seemed to have, daring to inch closer to her, "Hey Hawa, where is your home? Hey, Hawa, where is your husband? He-he-he . . . " I saw a boy get close to her and try to snatch her dupatta; she picked up a stone from the ground and ran after him. The boys quickly disappeared, scared by her sudden attack. She came back panting and sat in a corner eating a tomato she was given a few minutes earlier. She bit into the tomato and all the juices from the fruit dripped down her mouth and onto her hands and clothes.

On another visit to the market with my *nanape*, I saw Hawa again.

Somebody must have given her new clothes. She was excitedly showing off her outfit, giggling like a child: "Look I got a new dupatta . . .
it is blue . . . it is new . . . " She ate, drank, sat, and slept in those same
clothes. With time, they became faded, dirty and torn. As I watched
her in that dirty corner of the market, I wondered about Hawa's life.
Why was she wandering on the streets in a town where women were
rarely seen out? Hawa spoke Kutchi; her name was also a common
name among women in the Memon community. People understood
her to belong to this community. Women of the community wore a
burqa when they went out, if at all. I don't remember seeing Hawa in
a burqa. At that time, in my young mind, many questions emerged
for which I still seek answers.

A couple of years later, during yet another of my summer visits,
I heard that Hawa had had a baby. I was at the market with my aunt
and her daughter. The streets were busy, and the market was full of
people. When we reached the market, I scanned the scene for Hawa.
I asked my older cousin if she had seen her recently. She giggled and
whispered in my ear, for fear her mother might hear us talking about
such topics as baby-making, and get angry. "She had a baby. Some
government folks came and took Hawa and her baby with them
because people were complaining."

"But was she married?" I asked my cousin.

My cousin just shrugged her shoulders, reverting to nonverbal
communication as soon as she noticed her mother staring at her—a
sure sign that she needed to keep her mouth shut. All we knew as
children was that a woman had to be married to have a baby. So the
child in me wondered: how did mad Hawa have a baby? As children,
we found this very funny. We knew little about her and had only seen
her by herself. Hawa had had a baby, but she had no husband. How
funny!

My aunt Sayyeda once told me, when I was older, that many times
Hawa had sat in her front yard—the front compound as they call it in
India. She had given Hawa food and drink. She remembered Hawa
happily eating, smiling, and giggling as she ate. At times she fell

asleep right there in the yard. At other times, she ran out after eating quickly. My aunt said that from what she knew—from the meagre details she's gleaned between trying to talk to Hawa, and others from rumours that circulated—Hawa had been married off at the age of fourteen or fifteen. Parents in the community usually found husbands for their girls once they reached puberty. Sometimes they found a good young man in his twenties. Other times their daughters were wedded to older, divorced or widowed men. Girls didn't have a say in the matter. As the story goes, Hawa had been married to an older man in his forties. It was not clear how she had arrived in Upleta or where her family was from. People in Upleta had seen her on the streets for at least a couple of years. Nobody knew if her husband was still alive. Or if she was abused and had run away from her in-laws' house. Neither did anybody seem to know where Hawa spent her time when she was not around the market. My aunt said that at times in the darkness of night, people living in the far corners of the town heard screams and they thought it was Hawa having one of her fits. They would say, "Well, it must be that Hawa . . . keeps screaming in the middle of the night. For god's sake, Hawa, go to sleep and let us sleep . . ."

As I grew older and understood more, I kept wondering where Hawa had been taken. Where had she disappeared to? What happened to her? During my most recent trip to India in February 2018, I went to Upleta. It had been twenty years since I had last visited. As my taxi approached the borders of the town, I felt tears rolling down my cheeks—so many people dear to me, with whom I spent so much time in this town, were no longer in this world—my *nanape, nanima,* and a very dear maternal uncle, Hanif. Hanif's son, Armaan, is one of the nearest relatives I have who still lives in Upleta. Not wanting to venture out on my own, not knowing if I would be able to find my way around after a gap of two decades, I asked Armaan to accompany me to various places in the town. Our first stop was the vegetable market. It looked eerily unchanged—cows and goats roaming around, piles of vegetables, vendors competing to sell, floors made slippery by rotten vegetables and the water sprayed to keep produce fresh. I talked to a few of the salesmen and asked them if they knew anything about a woman named Hawa who used to sit in the market. Most of the merchants were young and did not know of such a woman. One man, who looked like he was in his forties, said he had heard of such a woman, but did not know or remember anything about her. All the people I talked to wondered why I, who to them appeared to be an outsider, was looking for information about Hawa. "Was she your relative?" one asked. Is she my relative, I wondered? How is one woman's story linked to another woman's? What sisterly solidarity do I feel with Hawa, who lived an exilic life in Upleta? All I am left with is to imagine Hawa's life. Like Virginia Woolf dreaming up Judith Shakespeare. Like Maxine Hong Kingston imagining her aunt. Women's lives—they exist only in so far as we imagine!

KATE RITTNER-WERKMAN

—⊃

Liebe Mutti, I Don't Mind Being German

In Alberta's capital city, back in the early 1970s, Edmonton's trendy Whyte Avenue was full of European shops stretching from 96 Street west as far as the eye could see.

Rain, snow, or shine, *meine Mutti und ich* would stroll down the avenue on Saturday mornings. It wasn't until years later that I realized the positive effect being in this neighbourhood had on my mother's mental health and why. As the aroma of European food filled the avenue air, German chatter did too.

Mutti was a brunette of unusual height and extraordinary beauty. At nineteen, she was modelling in her hometown of Hamburg, Germany, which is how she met my father, a tall blue-eyed handsome photographer.

"But he was married, so they had an affair," Oma, my mother's grandmother, told me one day as we sat on her green and brown speckled couch in front of dazzling lace curtains that parted the living room window, beyond which was a road called Schlegelsweg in Hamburg.

I learned that I was part of the ending to their story. Shortly after I was born, they were gone from each other and my father from me.

"And that's how you and your Mutti came to live with me," Oma said, all in German, of course. My parents divorced, and Mutti married my stepfather who flew us to our new life in Canada, much against her wishes. She went along with it anyway, thinking one day she would be able to return home to Hamburg.

Normally, Mutti was sad, pouty, and very moody especially after we settled in Edmonton for good. But one day, meine Mutti was buoyant. She was particularly lucid and kind. To me, her twelve-year-old daughter, it was a gift in time.

"Its like being back home," Mutti said to me, stepping onto Whyte Avenue in a clatter of heels. As the bus pulled away from the curb, she opened the shop door to the delicatessen, sounding the wind chimes, with me following quickly behind.

"Hallo, Hallo. Come and sit and enjoy the *Schwarzwälder kirschtorte*, a very special treat today," said the clerk, who had become one of my mother's only friends. She spoke English in a thick German accent, smiling and talking while serving the torte slices to us on imaginary plates of gold.

And enjoy, we did, while sipping aromatic *Kaffee* in cups steaming until the windows fogged.

The torte was a treat for me, but what was extra special was that I was allowed to drink steaming *Kaffee* with cream, which is how I like it to this day.

"Are you ready *mein Schatz*," Mutti said, reaching for my hand.

"*Einen shönen Tag noch*," she said turning to the shopkeepers. And we left the deli behind. Hand in hand, we were walking down the sunny avenue with a little bit of wind blowing, she in her blue knitted sweater and brown velvet hat, dark chocolate trim matching the colour of her eyes; and me in my blue French beret and blue uniform jacket, the one I am always wearing in childhood memories. But it's my mother that always stood out in the prairie streets—like she didn't quite fit. I was always in awe of her beauty, and she smelled of expensive perfume and fine leather.

There we were together, breathing in the avenue air on one of Alberta's finest of days 10,000 miles from home.

"Next stop—The House of Imports."

"*Sieh dir das an*," she said once inside. She pointed me to the

German magazines while we were listening to *Heintje* croon 'Mama' from invisible speakers, running our fingers and smoothing our hands over the textures of imported silks and textiles.

"Would you like to dance?" Mutti said, again taking my hand, twirling me, the awkward adolescent girl cringing with embarrassment and awe under her enchantment—me, her ugly duckling daughter, as she used to call me. That day, we were both white swans together in the bluest of ponds, timing the spaces between the porcelain-dish-stacked aisles, full of dolls and other finery.

"Stop! *Halt!*" the storekeeper said. And we did, giggling and laughing all the way to the next store.

For meine Mutti, speaking the language on our shopping trips to the avenue connected her to the well-known Hamburg boroughs of Altona, Eimsbuttel and Hamburg-Mitte which held the family and friends she had left behind, and where they still lived in the houses and apartments rebuilt from the rubble of the once allied-bombed streets. Those were the streets she grew up on against the backdrop of Nationalist Socialist Germany.

As difficult as it was, it was Mutti's culture. Her war and post-war culture. Born in 1938 it was all she knew. It was my father and stepfather's war and post-war culture too. In her marriage to my stepfather, she found he could never fill my father's shoes because he had different ones, which, in the end, my mother could not accept. And since many steps were taken in the dirt and mud and dust of us emerging into this Canadian landscape, I forgot about Hamburg and my father back in it. But my mother never did. He was everything to her, and yet she never spoke of him to me. As both of them had suffered war trauma—particularly my father who had been a soldier in that war—relationships were difficult to keep.

It's not easy to become part of a new culture, especially when carrying big suitcases of trauma across the sea. There are new customs to learn, a language barrier to overcome. And for German immigrants in particular, the lingering effect of the First World War and Second World War made coming into Canada difficult for a while.

On a whole, German-Canadians were better seen and not heard due to the ill will from the wars. In the sixties, without clusters of other German immigrants or family around her, Mutti became isolated and only grew more insecure, which impaired her ability to function within this new land, and her ability to be a parent.

As soon as I spoke English, starting in grade school, I learned all the reasons not to be German, not to be a part of this culture that Mutti came from; a place of an unforgivable war. I was fighting my condemned ethnicity with all I could, and with everything I learned from Hollywood anti-German movies and, of course, from social studies and neighbourhood kids. As a teenager, I rebelled against my Germaness and, as a young adult, I became a Canadian citizen disowned by Germany.

Then I finally found my father and called him on the phone. "I need to come home and see you," I said. But I did not wish to go back under a German passport.

After I arrived, my father asked me, "Would you like to come and live with me here by the Baltic Sea."

"No, thank you, it's too late. Canada is imprinted on me, the prairie land and bird song, and I am no longer a German citizen," I said. I showed him my new Canadian passport.

I was all of twenty-two then, the same age my mother was when she arrived in Canada.

In 1962 when I was three years old we flew away from Oma and the once war-torn Germany and landed at Toronto International Airport. We spent some time in Malton, Ontario, according to a document found in the family vault when my mother had to prove she had custody of me. My stepfather initiated this trip to Canada with a promise to my mother that if things did not work out in this wild land, she—or we—would be able to return home to Germany.

Once Ottawa cleared the documents proving that I belonged to my mother, we travelled west because my stepfather was in love with the Rockies. My mother however, was unhappy in Canada. Moving

first to Calgary, Alberta, which borders the Rocky Mountains and
their foothills, we lived for a while in a white house with a blue roof
surrounded by unfenced mountain grasses. Many tragedies happened
inside that house and even though it had windows, no one could
really see inside to rescue us. For one, I was four years old when a
baby girl was born to us in the fall of 1963.

And in the midst of the shadows of the Canadian winter disap-
pearing into spring, so did she. It happened so quickly I did not see
her crawl by me and out the door. By early1964 my sister was gone.
Away from us. How does a baby just disappear? I was four. I should
remember. After all, the neighbours remembered. Shortly after the
disappearance three of our neighbours were also asking this question
standing in front of our house on the sidewalk one sunny cool day. I
didn't see them until my mother told me about them. I was listening
to them.

"What happened to the baby?" the neighbour in a grey jacket was
asking the neighbour in a red dress and blue boots that matched our
roof.

"I don't know, was there just a baby in the house?" she said.

"You mean this white house with the blue roof had a baby in it? I
thought it just had Germans in it."

"What of the other child, the little German girl, is she still in
there? Look at her, she's in the window pointing her finger at us—
how rude—or is that a little boy? Hair is sure short enough!" said
the lady in the grey jacket.

My landed immigrant Mutti couldn't respond. There was a strong
accent on whatever English word she blurted out—a strong and rich
North German dialect rolling off her tongue sounding out the words
in a totally nonsensical fashion. And since my stepfather was on the
road selling Volkswagens, she could not manage or understand our
curious neighbours.

"I can't speak to them," Mutti said, but speaking to herself. "I can't
answer back, I can't explain. I can't explain to anyone," she said in
German walking back and forth feet pounding the floor. Suddenly she

stopped and looked down at me and wagged her finger in my face.

"Never tell anyone or I will throw you in the garbage can," she said it all in perfect German. And with that, she whipped the curtain closed on my nose.

She soon became afraid of the wild prairie land and all that roamed within it. And I became afraid of her.

But where the edge of the grasslands kissed the foothills was solice, my stepfather and I became enchanted with the wind, birds and rivers within the vast forests. He would take me on hikes to the mountain tops. My mother had never experienced anything like this, coming from a Hanseatic ocean city full of relatives and history and war and fish. Not beef, but fish and the odd pork hock.

The Free and Hanseatic City of Hamburg is one of the largest sea ports in Europe situated on rivers that take large ships such as tankers, merchant vessels, cruise ships out of the city port to the North and Baltic Seas. Hamburg has been around since the ninth century first as a castle and includes within it the history of one of my centuries old pirate grandfathers, Klaus Störtebeker, according to my father.

"Saxon inhabitants fought along side Störtebeker to defend the Hamburg castle against the likes of the Vikings, Dutch, Danish," he said on my visit with him.

Hamburg went on to be built on the sea and river waters and boasts more canals than Venice, as over two thousand bridges connect the residents of today who live mostly in harmony unless there is *Fußball* in St. Pauli.

In contrast, Edmonton is built on the flat prairies, a river city with flat roads, some rolling hills, farms, mountains off in the distance. No pirates here but cowboy gamblers riding wild horses through fields where one sees the strength of the wind in the lean of the light yellow shimmering grasses. This was all very new to Mutti. Unless you belonged to a church group of your culture, you were alone with it all. And she was. There were no English as a second language (ESL) programs.

"Return to Hamburg?" she asked my stepfather in 1964. But instead we moved further away, further west to the Pacific Ocean. "Maybe you will be happy by this sea," he said.

We packed up and drove out of Calgary without the baby in one of my stepfather's Volkswagens. We crossed the Rocky Mountains, arriving at the Pacific Ocean. But it was not like the North Sea. We lived in Port Coquitlam for a while, in a small grey house with a long driveway that curved up and around. The trees stood tall, the rocks were high. The landscape was different on the west coast of British Columbia where the air smelled of a musty ocean floating in seaweed forests; salty ship yards and deep salmon-crested rivers.

But no matter what was in the air or in the waters, tragedy followed us on the ground. Another baby was born in the summer of 1967 and was gone from our little grey house by the end of summer. And so were we. I was seven at the time.

This sister I had completely forgotten about until she came looking for relatives 40 years later, to remind us of her, only to leave us again when Mutti's story didn't suit her.

In 1968 we drove back to the Alberta prairies in a station wagon, briefly settling just north of Edmonton in St. Albert. Then off to Edmonton, settling in any neighbourhood that would have us, living in apartments on the south side close to Whyte Avenue where German Town was located. This small part of the Edmonton prairie city had been a lifeline for my mother, who had become, with each step, more unstable.

As the relationship between my mother and I changed, the avenue did too. Over time, new ethnic groups and businesses of all kinds moved into Whyte Avenue and took over many of the old German haunts. And even though the German consulate remains there, no one would ever know it was once an avenue full of European markets. There is no plaque that stands dedicated to the people or shops that once were there.

Thankfully, K&K Foodliner is still selling European goods such as teas, books, birthday cards, and meats like German garlic sausage.

And it's a place where I can eavesdrop on conversations in a rich language I once knew better. Customers discuss all of life's happenings in German while sussing out good schnitzel. It's here that one can pick up the latest copy of the *Albertaner*, a monthly German-language newspaper.

And Trinity Evangelical Lutheran Church, which still stands a block south of the avenue, tall on 100 Street, offers services in both German and English and houses the Historical Society of Germans in Poland and Volhynia, a library full of history, family stories and books and materials from the area. It is a golden find for German historical research, which I now do.

Through it all Mutti and I had become estranged to the point that I missed her death. I found out she died when I went to find her at her last place of known residence to tell her that I now understood all of it—her life and my father's life. It was her landlord who told me she had passed away. By then my stepfather had left her.

A public trustee took care of Mutti's funeral arrangements and was working the case. I found out the trustee's office tried to reach me but failed, since the office does not conduct out-of-province name searches, and I had married outside of Alberta and changed my surname. The trustee's office did find the one baby girl now grown and living in Germany. But she didn't know what to do and had washed her hands of Mutti after all, she had faked her death once.

Yet to the public trustee none of this applied. She wanted to grant Mutti's one last wish, which Mutti had handwritten on a swath of paper: *My body is to be cremated and my ashes sent back to Neuer Friedhof Hamburg-Harburg. Under no circumstances will I be buried in Canada.*

"Your mother's case affected me deeply. Our office is not allowed to act without first contacting relatives, but as none were forthcoming I went ahead with the cremation. I wanted to fulfill her final wish of returning to Germany," the trustee said. She had then contacted the offices of Canada's Consulate General of Germany to please arrange to take Mutti's ashes home because upon her death, she was still a German citizen.

"But they refused," the trustee said. Instead the woman who as a child had survived the allied fire bombing of Hamburg in 1943 during the Second World War is interned in a cemetery east of Edmonton close to the red maple leaf which waves over the Field of Honour, where protective Canadian soldiers are laid to rest.

Meine Mutti's ashes are mixed with the fertile Canadian prairie farmland, the one she could never embrace. Here in the fall the small hills are covered in billowing sunflowers and the prairie summer winds can blow strong and warm and soft against the skin, yet hard enough to take the very landscape with it. And the crisp winter wind can freeze its path in an instant, burning the landscape in glittering forever frost.

I discovered after her death that Mutti suffered from borderline personality disorder. With this unwittingly in her mind she had unpacked her suitcases, the ones full of trauma, as a young woman in a new country. That is what ailed her and us, all our lives together. It is what drove us apart.

"The cause of her BPD being mostly environmental, from what she experienced as a young child during the war," her psychiatrist said.

I long for those days of German Town, and to walk with her again down the avenue. To dance with her, if only to speak German with her and relay what I now know. Which isn't really much more than I knew then. Except, I would say, "Mutti, I don't mind being German. Becoming Canadian allowed me to embrace it."

Liebe Mutti, Es Macht Mir Nichts Aus, Deutsch Zu Sein

In den späten sechziger Jahren war die jetzt trendy 82. Avenue (Whyte Avenue) voller deutscher Händler. Ihre Läden erstreckten sich westlich zwischen der 96. und der 104. Straße. Man konnte deutsche Filme finden, Restaurants, Feinkostgeschäfte, Spielzeugläden, Rechtsanwälte, Uhr- und Schuhmacher, Bäckereien und Tuchwarenhändler. Alles sehr nah' bei einander.

Ich nannte die Gegend „German Town".

Meine Mutter – Mutti - und ich sind bei Regen, Schnee und Sonnenschein die Straße der German Town auf- und abgegangen. Meistens samstags morgens. Erst viel später habe ich erkannt, wie positiv sich der Besuch in der Gegend auf die Psyche meiner Mutter auswirkte - und was der Grund dafür war. So wie das urtümliche Aroma von Lebkuchen, Franzbrötchen und Knoblauchwürsten die Luft erfüllte, tat es das deutsche Geplauder auch.

Wir haben bei Erikas Feinkostladen vorbeigeschaut, geredet und zwei oder drei Stück Buttercremetorte gegessen. Der nächste Zwischenstopp war „The House of Imports", um die neuesten Zeitschriften durchzublättern, deutsche Musik von zu Hause zu hören, importierte Stoffe zu befühlen und durch die angebotenen Haushaltswaren die deutsche Kultur zu riechen, die wir verloren hatten. In „Charley's German Meat and Sausage" Metzgerei habe ich zugehört und heimlich ein Stückchen Wurst probiert, während meine Mutter noch einmal die Nachrichten diskutierte, dieses Mal in Verbindung mit der Frage: „Was ist heute der beste Tagespreis, und für welches Fleisch gilt er?" Alles auf deutsch. Und glauben Sie mir, wenn Sie bei diesem Metzger Frikadellen bestellten, wusste der ganz genau, was gemeint war. Weitere Erklärungen waren nicht nötig, er mischte die verschiedenen Fleischsorten, so wie Mutti es gewohnt war.

Für meine Mutter, die jede Verbindung zu ihrer Heimat verloren hatte, bedeutete das Sprechen der Sprache einzig und allein während der Einkaufstouren in „German Town" eine Verbindung zu den ihr wohlbekannten Stadtteilen Hamburgs - Altona, Eimsbüttel, Hamburg-Mitte, wo noch immer Familie und Freunde lebten, die sie in Deutschland zurückgelassen hatte.

Teil einer neuen Kultur zu werden, ist nicht leicht für Flüchtlinge, Einwanderer und „landed immigrants" (Einwanderer mit ständiger Aufenthaltsgenehmigung). Man muss sich an die Sitten und Gebräuche der neuen Kultur gewöhnen, Sprachbarrieren überwinden und andere Probleme lösen, die für Einwanderer, die vor langer Zeit ankamen, einfach zu verstehen schienen. Und dann gibt es noch die Art und Weise, wie die Menschen miteinander umgehen, wie die eigene Kultur respektiert wird im Vergleich zu der neuen Kultur.

Besonders für deutsche Einwanderer machten die anhaltenden Folgen der zwei Weltkriege das Ankommen in der kanadischen Kultur schwer. Ohne Anschluss an Gruppen anderer deutscher Einwanderer oder Familien in der Umgebung waren wir eine unsichtbare Minderheit, die man besser sieht (als Arbeitskräfte) als hört, wegen der anhaltenden Feindseligkeit aufgrund der Kriege. Sobald ich Englisch lernte, erfuhr ich - schon ab der Grundschule - alles über die Gründe, nicht deutsch sein zu wollen. Als Teenager habe ich dann angefangen, gegen Deutschland und das Deutschsein zu rebellieren. Das stand direkt im Widerspruch zum Bedürfnis meiner Mutter, deutsch zu sein und eines Tages nach Deutschland zurückzukehren.

Meine Mutter, mein Stiefvater und ich kamen im Herbst 1962 von Deutschland aus in Kanada an. Nur zwölf Jahre zuvor hatte die kanadische Einwanderungsbehörde die Deutschen von der Liste der feindlichen Ausländer gestrichen.

Von Hamburg gestartet, landeten wir auf dem Lester B. Pearson Flughafen in Toronto. Wir verbrachten einige Zeit in der Gegend, wo meine Mutter beweisen musste, dass sie das Sorgerecht für mich hatte. Das weiß ich aus einem Dokument, das ich nach ihrem Tod gefunden habe. Mein Stiefvater hatte die Reise initiiert - mit dem Versprechen an meine Mutter, dass sie oder wir nach Hause nach Deutschland zurückkehren könnten, wenn die Dinge in diesem wilden Land nicht gut liefen. Aber das sollte nicht der Fall sein. Mein Stiefvater, der aus Köln stammte, verliebte sich in die Rocky Mountains und war entschlossen, ein Leben in Kanada aufzubauen -weg von seiner Familie in Deutschland.

Nachdem Ottawa die Dokumente anerkannt hatte, die zeigten, dass ich zu meiner Mutter gehörte, reisten wir nach Westen.

Zunächst zogen wir für eine Weile nach Calgary, das an die Ausläufer der Rocky Mountains grenzt. Als ein Schicksalsschlag unsere kleine Familie traf, wollte meine Mutter weg. Da sie kein Englisch konnte und mein Stiefvater viel und lange unterwegs war, um Volkswagen zu verkaufen, konnte sie weder mit den neugierigen Nachbarn umgehen noch sie verstehen. Sie bekam Angst vor der wilden Prärie, den nördlichen Ebenen und allem, was darin kreuchte und fleuchte. So viele Tiere, die sie noch nie gesehen hatte, die Kälte, der Wind, die Indianer, die Sitten und Gebräuche.

Da, wo sich die Ränder der Graslandschaften mit den Gebirgsausläufern vereinen und zu Bergwäldern werden, waren mein Stiefvater und ich wie verzaubert von den Winden und den Wäldern. Er hat mich häufig auf seine Wanderungen zu den Berggipfeln mitgenommen. Meine Mutter hatte so etwas noch nie erlebt, da sie aus einer Hansestadt am Meer kam, einer Stadt der Freunde und Verwandten, voller Geschichte, Krieg und Fisch. Nicht Rindfleisch, Fisch. Aus einer Gegend, wo die Küche hauptsächlich aus Fisch und Meeresfrüchten bestand.

Schließlich liegt Hamburg an der Elbe, die in die Nordsee mündet. Die Stadt gilt als das Tor zur Welt. Durch die Stadtmitte verläuft die Alster; und viele Kanäle und Brücken verbinden den Stadtverkehr.

Im Gegensatz dazu ist Alberta ein Prärieland, und daher war alles neu und fremd für sie; diese befremdliche Provinz mit Hügellandschaften, flachem Farmland, Flüssen und Seen und Wind, der einen umhauen kann – wo viel Mais angebaut wird und wo im Spätsommer hohe Sonnenblumen blühen. Es waren die frühen sechziger Jahre. Wenn man nicht Teil einer Kirchengemeinde seiner eigenen Kultur war, war man mit allem allein. Es gab keine Kurse für Erwachsene, um Englisch als Zweitsprache zu erlernen; und das „Edmonton Mennonite Center for Newcomers" gab es noch nicht.

Zurück nach Hamburg? Sie fragte meinen Stiefvater. Doch statt dessen zogen wir noch weiter weg, weiter nach Westen, an den Pazifik – den Stillen Ozean. „Vielleicht wirst du an diesem Meer glücklich", sagte mein Stiefvater.

Also verschwanden wir in einer Winternacht aus Calgary und überquerten die Rocky Mountains, die wir bestiegen hatten, und kamen an den Pazifik. Aber es war ein anderer Ozean. Es war nicht die Nordsee. Für eine Weile lebten wir in Port Coquitlam. Als uns ein weiterer Schicksalsschlag traf, fuhren wir zurück in die Prärie Albertas. Wir ließen uns in St. Albert, nördlich von Edmonton, nieder. Doch der Drang umzuziehen, immer wenn etwas Schlimmes passierte, begleitete uns weiterhin. So zogen wir nach Edmonton, wo wir willkommen waren. Wir lebten in Wohnungen im Süden, in der Nähe der Whyte Avenue und „German Town".

In der Zwischenzeit waren neue Völkergruppen und Geschäfte verschiedener Art in die Whyte Avenue gezogen und hatten viele der deutschen Stätten übernommen. Heute würde niemand ahnen, dass dies einmal „German Town" war, voll mit deutschen Händlern, die deutsche Waren verkauften. Es gibt auch keine Plakette, die an diese Zeit erinnert.

Zum Glück gibt es noch K&K Foodliner in der Whyte Avenue, wo es deutsche Waren wie Geschichtsbücher, Geburtstagskarten, Tees und Fleischwaren wie deutsche Knoblauchwurst zu kaufen gibt. Es ist ein Ort, an dem ich Gesprächen lauschen kann in einer so reichen Sprache, die ich einmal besser konnte. Deutsche, die alles auf deutsch diskutieren, während sie die Vorzüge eines guten Schnitzels unter die Lupe nehmen. Hier kann man auch die neueste Ausgabe des „Albertaner" bekommen, einer monatlich erscheinenden deutschen Zeitung.

Es muss also hier noch Deutsche geben. Auf jeden Fall in der „Trinity Evangelical Lutheran Church", die einen Block südlich der Whyte Avenue auf der 100. Straße steht und wo Gottesdienste sowohl auf Deutsch als auch auf Englisch abgehalten werden. Hier findet man auch die Bibliothek der „Historical Society of Germans in Poland and Volhynia", einer Bibliothek voller Geschichte, Familiengeschichten und Büchern und Materialien aus der Gegend. Eine Fundgrube für Forschung zur deutschen Geschichte.

Was mich angeht, ich wurde Reporterin bei einer Zeitung in einer kleinen Stadt in Alberta, die über Ereignisse in der Gemeinde, wie zum Beispiel die Feierlichkeiten zum „Remembrance Day", schreibt und sie fotografiert.

Ich habe zwei tolle Kinder hier in Edmonton großgezogen. Beide haben ein reiches Wissen über ihr deutsch-holländisches Erbe. Ich habe mit ihnen Deutsch gesprochen, als sie klein waren, aber da ich niemanden hatte, mit dem ich sprechen konnte, war das auf die Dauer schwierig. Und doch hat es in ihnen ein Bewusstsein für ihre deutsche Kultur geweckt, und sie haben an der Universität weiter Deutsch gelernt.

Aber meine Mutter und ich haben uns entfremdet. Sie ist gestorben und liegt östlich von Edmonton begraben, wo der Boden aus fruchtbarem Farmland besteht, inmitten von Hobbypferdefarmen und Ländereien, wo im Herbst die kleinen Hügel von wogenden Sonnenblumen überflutet sind. Hier können die Präriewinde warm und weich über die Haut streichen, aber auch stark genug wehen, um die fruchtbare Erde wegzublasen; wo die beißende Winterluft in nur einem Moment gefriert, während sie die Landschaft in ein wunderschönes Märchenland verzaubert.

Muttis Asche ist jetzt vermischt mit der Erde dieser kanadischen Landschaft, die sie nie annehmen konnte.

Ich sehne mich manchmal nach der Zeit von „German Town" und danach, wieder mit Mutti die Whyte Avenue hinunterzulaufen. Von der dekadenten Torte in Erikas Feinkostgeschäft bis zum Verweilen im „House of Imports", noch einmal ein Lächeln auf ihren Lippen zu sehen.

Wenn auch nur, um noch einmal mit ihr auf Deutsch zu sprechen und ihr mitzuteilen, was ich heute weiß. Was nicht wirklich viel mehr ist als das, was ich damals wusste.

Außer, dass ich sagen würde: „Mutti, es macht mir nichts mehr aus, deutsch zu sein. Kanadierin zu werden, hat es mir erlaubt, mein Deutschsein anzunehmen."

Author's Note

A country's cultural identity is only as strong as its folklore. And Canadians are struggling with their identity as a country, which makes our memoir kind of hard to define.

Yet, through the eyes of a white settler and German Heritage speaker, I tell stories reflecting my own biography within this Canadian landscape that surrounds me. The strongest connection I feel is to the places where my children took their first breaths.

My son, born in Victoria, British Columbia, carries the West Coast spirit within him. When he was young, I would place him in a carrier and take him to the ocean side during the wind storms. With my baby on my back I would stand so he could watch waves crash into the shore of Roberts Bay, showering us in divine sea-salt spray. He would giggle his glorious giggle. And I remember us sitting on the cliffs of the Saanich Inlet waters listening to the drums of the West Coast Salish echoing earth songs on the seascape.

The newspaper business carried us north from Victoria. Soon after our arrival my daughter was born in Yellowknife, Northwest Territories. She carries the strength of the Northern spirit within her. Through my gathering of Northern stories, I was invited to a Dene sweat but I couldn't attend because I was pregnant. The Elder who invited me blessed my baby in utero with an eagle feather. In this place of long dark winter, I made a dreamcatcher with my doula out of the willow branches we collected in the frosty spring light. Soon after the sun became tethered to the moon as the height of Northern summer approached, my daughter was born and the dreamcatcher bloomed.

My children's first breaths joined them to this undefined Canadian mosaic, and if you listen closely, the stories told from coast to coast to coast, whether written, painted, sculpted, totemed, danced, filmed, and whether fictional or not, are a whisper of what our cultural identity is.

And we Canadians want to own a piece of it, because we see our reflections in these stories, this possible identity. We want to feel it, become part of it, wear it, define it, taste it. But instead, we fight over it, like a broken family wanting to get back together again, seeing the vision but not knowing quite how to get there.

—

"Liebe Mutti, es macht mir nichts aus, deutsch zu sein" was translated by Eva Guenther, PhD.

LEILEI CHEN

———⊃

Life Begins at Forty

Clearly, I was feeling nostalgic. I was sitting at my desk in Edmonton, organizing a pile of old family photographs from China. And I was waiting for my inkstone tea tray to arrive in the mail. Before moving to Canada in 2004, I had never heard of inkstone tea trays. They would have been condemned as *si jiu* (四旧) in the Cultural Revolution—the Four Olds referring to old culture, old ideas, old customs, and old habits—and doomed for destruction. Now they were becoming popular with the revival of tea culture in China. Usually in an uneven oval shape, they are exquisitely carved from the same material people use to grind inksticks with water to generate ink for Chinese calligraphy. An inkstone tea tray sets the stage for a tea ceremony. You lay out the little tea cups, the little tea pot, and the little tea pets that symbolize good fortune. You pour hot water over all these little objects on the tea tray to warm them up, and then you fill the warm cups with tea. The tea tray I bought was made of *lü duan yan* (绿端砚), light green in colour and the only one of its kind in China. In the green were different shades of yellow and brown. The sculptor had crafted it out of the natural stone and named it *ping hu qiu yue* (平湖秋月)—Mirror Lake, Autumn Moon.

I had never taken interest in such old-fashioned Chinese art before, and my own eagerness surprised me. The tray was heavy—forty-four kilos—and I shipped it all the way from Guangzhou. I had never bothered to look through old family photos before, either.

When had I become interested in looking back? After all these years in Canada, I must be getting old.

I held in my hand a black-and-white photo taken when I was fourteen. I gasped at how far I had travelled. The girl in the picture looked no more than ten. She was pale and small. She sat cross-legged in a foldable armchair, earnestly reading a magazine. A little chick foraged under the chair. Behind the girl was the rugged earthen wall of a rural residence. The picture reminded me of what travel writers would call a poor, backward countryside. But it was not poor or backward to me. It brought back my happiest memories: that summer holiday when I went with my sister to visit our grandparents in rural Anhui.

It was 1984. I was in grade seven and my sister in grade five. Road trips were rare, and a two-hour bus ride from Suzhou (宿州) to Gaolou (高楼) was an adventure. We lived in a small town, and the countryside was a wonderland to us. The vast fields outside the bus window were exhilarating. I wanted to learn the names of all the plants—wheat, corn, watermelons, yams. I always admired the kids who could name the grasses and wildflowers. I loved walking in the fields with my auntie. It was a delight to discover that peanuts grow in the soil. Not on a bush or a tree but literally under the ground. And my pride when I learned to fertilize the corn field! Following my auntie, I dug a little hole about two inches away from the plant, scooped in the fertilizer there, and then covered the hole up. "The plant will surely yield more corn this fall," she said, smiling at me. I was thrilled that I had done a thing of such importance.

I looked serious in the photo. Eventually, that seriousness would become ambition. Already I was completely mesmerized by English. "How wonderful it would be if I could communicate with foreigners in *their* language!" I thought to myself.

Wasn't I always the little girl who dreamed about seeing the larger world out there? I remembered doing homework at the desk in my childhood home in Suzhou (宿州). It was a rectangular-shaped single room but functioned as a living room, a bedroom, a study, a dining room, and a semi-kitchen in wintertime. My desk faced the window that opened to a dead-end narrow lane on both sides. Every time I heard a train chugging and whistling past the railway station nearby, I dreamed of riding it to the world out there, a world that must be full of novelty, excitement, and wonder.

I decided that English would be my major and chose the arts stream for the last two years of high school. This shocked everyone—my teachers, my classmates, and my parents. Smart kids were supposed to study science. The saying went, "Learn maths, physics, and chemistry well, and you'll travel the world without fear." I chose to study English anyway, completed my undergraduate and master's program with flying colours, and became a professor of English. I had no fear travelling the world.

Now looking at this girl in the picture taken more than three decades ago, I couldn't believe I had travelled so far. The skinny girl in the picture could never imagine she would live in Edmonton, Canada. She didn't know Edmonton existed.

I put aside the photo and looked out at the backyard garden of my Edmonton home. The purple and pink lupines nodding their heads to me felt like a dream.

The next photo was taken in the summer of 1992. Guang embraced me from behind, both of us smiling widely at the camera. Behind was the lake of Yaohai Park (瑶海公园) laced with lush willow trees, forming a peaceful backdrop for the picture. Looking at this beautiful couple, who could know their love was once forbidden?

I was in the fourth year of university and ready to begin my master's degree when I met Guang. At a university party, he asked me to dance. We danced until the end of the evening and never changed partners. We started dating, but no one believed he was a good match for me. I was nerdy, shy, and anonymous, sociable only on Thursday afternoons when the English corner on campus was open for people to practice oral English. Guang was visible. He was tall, muscular, and physically attractive. He played soccer shirtless with a bunch of

students who were also shirtless. He was a Physical Education professor and the admired coach of the university men's handball team.
He was the head organizer of the university's annual sports meetings.
And he was a rebel. When the head of the general affairs office called
the Phys Ed profs "a gang of rascals," Guang literally threw him in
his down jacket into the hot public bathing pool.

China's welfare housing system in the late 1980s couldn't offer
everyone a decent home, and Guang, a Phys Ed prof in Anhui University, slept in a storage room next to the department office. Many
junior professors remained similarly homeless. But the senior officials
had both off-campus apartments and private rooms on campus where
they could nap after lunch. After two years of sleeping in the storage
room on a flimsy foldable bed, surrounded by boxes of shot, javelin
piles, and pommel horses, Guang rolled up his bamboo mat one day
and knocked at the university president's door after lunchtime.

The door opened and the president greeted Guang with sleepy eyes.
"President Tsai," Guang said. His tone was respectful. "Sorry, I don't
mean to disrupt your nap, but something urgent has come up."

"Who are you? What do you want?" President Tsai was obvi-
ously annoyed.

"I'm a professor in the Phys Ed Department currently living in
the storage room. I have been there for two years."

"Well, young man, you're not alone," President Tsai replied.
"Lots of young teachers have the same difficulty and have been waiting for better housing longer than you, and they are still waiting."
Guang's complaint was not new. The president thought he could
easily dismiss this one as he had the others.

"Well, I'm not asking for my own room. I'm just asking to share a
bit of your on-campus room," Guang cheekily replied. "Let me toss
my mat beside your bed for a few hours' sleep at night, when you're
not even there, and the room is yours during the day. I won't ever
bother you again."

President Tsai was totally unprepared for such insolence. He was
dumbfounded, his face turning red and hands trembling. "You . . .

you . . . how dare you!" His lips quivering and fingers pointing. He grabbed the glass on the table beside him and smashed it with great force, the tea spilling as the broken pieces fell on the floor.

Guang ultimately got his room on campus. And a reputation for challenging authority.

Upon hearing this story, Professor Wu warned me, "You should reconsider your relationship with him. I heard he's impetuous." Professor Wu was a senior prof and very well respected. She treated me like her own daughter, and I knew she meant well.

"I think he is courageous." My retort surprised me, but I couldn't stop myself. "He has a strong sense of justice. His colleagues like him, and his students absolutely adore him!"

My father, who had always been proud of his daughter, was never so disappointed as when he learned I had "a sports club" boyfriend (体育棒子)—a Chinese slang for a jock. He asked me, quietly seething, "How much do you think you know him? Do you know how old he is?"

"He is thirty. He loves me and I love him. That's enough!" Dating a strange man eight years older than me who moved in different circles was completely outrageous to my father.

Later, I would be inspired by George Eliot's elopement with a married man in Victorian England. At that point, I hadn't heard of her yet. But if elopement had been necessary, I would have done it in an instant.

Jin, my best friend since Grade 7, was not encouraging either. "He doesn't suit you. You need a scholar. Someone like you."

"Really? I think Guang is so attractive. I like to have an outspoken and lively person around me. And he does love books. He has an amazing knowledge of human history," I said, trying to convince my best friend that mine was not an infatuation.

We laughed about those moments when I visited my father, Professor Wu, and Jin on my homecoming trip in 2011. My father said that Guang not only stole his daughter's heart but melted his as well.

Guang joined China's pursuit of prosperity. In 1992 he started to work in the international transportation business in the southern city of Guangzhou, the exciting frontier of China's economic reform. We settled in Guangzhou, and a whole new world opened up to me. I was twenty-five years old.

Guangzhou was everything that Anhui wasn't. It sprawled. Everywhere I looked I saw prosperity, excitement, and possibility. The Garden Hotel, White Swan Hotel, and the sixty-three-storey World Trade Centre. The boutiques lining both sides of the Beijing Road, the Xin Da Xin (新大新), the Friendship Department Store stuffed with goods. People in business suits walking in and out of glass-sided office buildings. The colourful blossoms, the palm trees and banyans, the weather so warm that I could wear pretty dresses all year round—it felt like paradise.

"Buying pretty clothes won't be a problem anymore!" Before, I had searched every corner of Suzhou in Anhui with my grandma for a light coat but couldn't find one I liked. I needed it badly, and Grandma had promised it to me as a birthday gift. I could have bought one if I had been less picky. But I would rather not wear a coat than have one I didn't like. Suzhou was a small town in Anhui with limited choices. Guangzhou's abundance seemed boundless. I was in heaven.

The first bite of watermelon in a fancy Guangzhou karaoke bar felt so luxurious! It was the dead of winter and I was eating a delicious summer fruit! The chill in my bones from Hefei's winter instantly dissolved. I felt like a royal, like Yang Guifei, the Tang Dynasty emperor's favorite concubine enjoying the lychee brought by speedy horsemen all the way from Canton to Chang'an.

But in Guangzhou I also felt like an immigrant. Local people spoke Cantonese; I spoke Mandarin. It was funny to think I could understand English from the Voice of America or BBC but not Cantonese from my own city. Mandarin was China's official language, but my students at Jinan University came from Hong Kong, Macau, Southeast Asia, and other overseas Chinese communities around the world, and spoke mostly Cantonese. I decided to learn Cantonese in order to communicate with my students better. I had learned English in a school setting, but I learned Cantonese from people around me and by using it in my daily life. It led me to a new way of life: *yim tsa* (去茶楼喝茶), or tea-drinking, meant eating at a Chinese dim sum restaurant; *hang fa gai* (春节逛花市) meant shopping for flowers in the town during the Spring Festival; and *bao lao fuo tang* (煲老火汤) referred to cooking different herbal broths nearly every day in the different seasons of the year. I "lived" the dialect by enjoying the Cantonese way of life.

Guangzhou was my home. I became a professor of English, I gave birth to a daughter and started a family, and I helped my parents and sister move and settle there. In Guangzhou I became resilient and strong. I lived there for only nine years, a short time. Yi-Fu Tuan, the humanist geographer, said that one's attachment to a place did not necessarily relate to how long one had stayed there. And what mattered to me was the broad life experience Guangzhou offered. The experience of learning a new language and growing with the nutrients of a new way of life.

Ah, the angel of the hearth. In this photo, my long, white dress was spread wide and took up the lower half of the picture. I was sitting beside a fireplace, holding a bouquet of artificial red roses and smiling at the camera. This was one of my favorite professional studio photos. Thirty years later, youth, elegance, and joy still glowed from it.

"I look like the ideal Victorian woman. An Angel at the Hearth," I had mocked myself when I began to feel unhappy about my role in the family. After Sarah was born, my life became absorbed with petty motherly duties, while Guang became increasingly successful in his business and less present at home.

Years before, Guang and I had sat on a cafe patio extending into Xiyuan Lake on the edge of our university campus, sipping ice tea and dreaming about our future. Guang had pictured me sitting beside a fireplace, reading a Victorian novel.

"You'll be a great scholar, a gentle wife, and a loving mother," he said. Andy Williams's "Love Story" song in the background. The glittering surface of the lake. The starry sky above. I was intoxicated by the certainty in his voice.

We both believed it was the perfect arrangement for our future: Guang would build our wealth and I would teach in a university and, with my flexible schedule, look after our home. I wouldn't have considered being a professor before that; in the early 1990s, a university professor in China earned less than a roasted-yam peddler in the street. I wanted a decent income and hoped my English proficiency would bring me work in a foreign company or at least a joint venture. Everyone wanted a well-paying job back then. But I ended up being a professor nevertheless. Guang could make us rich. Together, we would have a perfect family.

And then Sarah was born. I continued to win teaching awards, get research funds, and get promoted, but I felt miserable. Guang's seat was almost always empty at the dinner table. He needed to dine with his business associates. Dinners led to singing, dancing, drinking, gambling at a karaoke bar, and then to a de-stressing massage at a sauna house. At home, I picked up Sarah from school, fed her supper, put her to bed, told her bedtime stories, and then, after she fell asleep, worked on my own writing and research while waiting for Guang. He rarely came home before midnight. The next morning when I cooked breakfast, fed and dressed Sarah, and sent her to school, Guang would be still asleep.

I felt like a single mom. My daughter barely saw her dad. Discontent grew like a disease.

"I'm like Laura in *The Hours*." Laura was an unhappy housewife always alone at home with a young child and pregnant with a baby, while her husband came and went in his business suit. She fulfilled the standard of being an angel in the house, but it depressed her to the point of attempted suicide. The Victorian ideal had become unreal and strange to me.

I smiled at the naïveté of that young Leilei in the photo. I used to blame Guang for endorsing patriarchy and taking care of the family only at the financial level. Was I not the same? Hadn't I enabled it by promising to be his gentle wife and supporting him wholeheartedly? Later, in Edmonton, I realized that I had been unfair. I had blamed Guang for my own discontent.

I decided to pursue an English PhD away from home. The life of a gentle wife and a dutiful mother had nothing for me. Guang didn't want me to go. I knew that. But he didn't ask me to stay. He had always supported my scholarly endeavours. He had urged me to do a master's degree in Hefei, even though it meant staying three years apart.

And now a PhD. When I showed him the letter from the University of Alberta in Edmonton offering entrance and a prestigious scholarship, Guang was calm. As if he had already known. I knew he didn't want me to leave him and Sarah behind.

Shortly after my first Christmas, Sarah called me from China.

"Mummy, you know what? Dad has a biiiiiig birthday surprise for you. You're going to love it!"

"Oh, yes? Tell me what. I'll keep it a secret. I won't tell Dad you told me."

"I can't, Mummy. I promised him we'd keep it a secret until your birthday. But you're going to love it, for sure!"

It was Guang who broke the promise. He couldn't hold the secret any longer and phoned me one day to say that he had bought a huge, luxurious penthouse by the Pearl River for my birthday. A private elevator led from the underground parking lot straight up to the living room. Through the phone I could feel his longing. He wanted me to come back badly.

Later, when Guang sold this penthouse and brought Sarah with him to Edmonton, when he managed to buy a house here, when he started his car business from scratch in this foreign place without knowing the language, and when he began to learn English, I knew the love between us was still alive, nice and warm like the flickering fire in the photo.

But the Angel of the Hearth was finally dead.

The last photo was taken at Guangzhou Flower City Square in 2011. I was walking towards the camera, awestruck at the other side of the Flower City Square, a complex that didn't exist before. The Canton Tower, Guangdong Museum, Guangzhou Public Library, Guangzhou Opera House, Guangzhou No. 2 Children's Palace, *Haixinsha* (海心沙) or Sand in the Ocean Park, and a myriad of glittering skyscrapers. The folded umbrella in my hand indicated that I was a Guangzhouer; like anyone who lived here, I carried it wherever I went to protect against both sun and rain. But my shameless gaze and the naked wonder at the modernity, at the new alien growth, flagged me as an outsider. A stranger in my home city.

The stark materialism of the 1990s and the 2000s was to be expected after a century of poverty. A century of the Manchus' rule, Western colonization, Japanese invasion, the Civil War, and the Communist revolutions. But the cost—important artistic and historic cultural sites demolished in favour of modernization and wealth—had troubled me deeply, even though Guang and I had participated in China's pursuit of wealth. Even though prosperity had felt so necessary to us. But here, in the Flower City Square, the museum, the library, the children's palace, and the opera house all gestured to the artistic and the cultural. They mattered to China once again.

Above, clouds floated in Guangzhou's blue sky. In 1993 and in 2008 the soupy pollution had made me sick. Now the air was fresh, clear, exhilarating. This was my home, a place where I had lived for nine years. The place where I built my family, raised my daughter, established my career, and learned independence. I was thrilled to again enjoy the delicious food in Guangzhou's restaurants, the hospitality, the warm climate, the prosperity, energy, and liveliness of the city.

But I was also looking forward to going back to my other home. I had bonded to Edmonton. I missed the quiet reading hours with Guang and Sarah by the fireplace, Apple purring on my lap; I loved hiking in the Wedgewood Ravine near our house; I loved the enlightening and inspiring conversations with people at the university; I loved laughing and talking with my friends in both the English and Chinese reading clubs . . .

I set the photos aside and looked out the window. I felt contented now. With China. With Edmonton. With who I am. As peaceful as the mirror lake of my tea tray.

Confucius said one has no doubts upon reaching forty. Truly, he was a wise man. "Life begins at forty," I murmured. The doorbell rang. My tea tray had arrived.

Author's Note

I feel agitated if I don't write. During the past twenty years of academic life in China and Canada, I have written research papers and my writing has been dictated by the institution of academia. Only after I settled in the new country did I realize that writing can be the most liberating activity.

Now I write to express myself. Since moving to Edmonton, I have been keeping an English journal. Writing becomes a place where I engage with my second language, make sense of who I am in this new culture, and find peace during moments of hardship and adversity.

The Borderlines Writers Circle program of the Writers' Guild of Alberta invited me into a writers' community and here, in this community, I feel a growing sense of responsibility. Each settler in this country has a story to tell, whether it is about coming in a boat from England or Vietnam, or escaping from the war in Germany or Russia. It is the diversity of the individual stories—of both the settlers and the Indigenous groups—that matters. Coming from my home country to Canada and having built my new home here, I feel obligated to tell mine.

So I write.

SHIMELIS GEBREMICHAEL

⟶

When Weather Talks Loud

1. Broken Promises

Except hope, except thought / The future is always secret
—S Gebremichael

"Shime," my friend Menigistu shouts across the crowded, buzzing room. He uses my nickname, and I shout back, "Menge!" We have often remarked that he has the same name—Menigistu Halemariam—as one of the leaders of the Communist era in Ethiopia, the turbulent years from 1970 to 1990 when Menge and I were growing up. We make our way towards each other and he grips my shoulder to get my full attention. "See my lovely feet? You remember that they are size 9 ½, right?" He grins.

"Yes . . . how about them?"

"So, when you get to Canada and start to grab dollars, remember your old friend here. Adidas would be great, but Nike will work just as well."

I am in the middle of a gathering in my home city, Addis Ababa, to celebrate my life-altering decision to immigrate to Canada. My wonderful aunt, Ehite Meles, whom I have always called Mami, has orchestrated this evening in a spectacular way to make my last supper delightful and unforgettable. I am simmering within the smells, tastes and colours of festivity. The taste of *kitfo*, a beloved Ethiopian dish of minced raw beef mixed with spices and butter, fills my senses. I am overcome with nostalgia, knowing that it will be a long while before I am able to return to my homeland. Mellowness envelops me as I enjoy *tella*, traditional Ethiopian beer, and *tej*, a rich honey wine. I am grateful for the efforts my aunt Ehite has gone through, to make this gathering a success. Since I lost my own mother seven years ago, Mami has become even more important and beloved to me. She is one of the *Habesha*, a collective name given to Ethiopian and Eritrean women who cheer people when they visit their home, and invite guests to eat and drink. Mami is in her mid-fifties, with the typical features of an Ethiopian mother. She has a warm brown complexion and a friendly, open face. She likes dressing professionally, probably because she worked for four decades as a secretary. But above all, she enjoys the companionship of her family, neighbours, and friends.

It is hardly possible to see her house without a congregation at least once a week. And for me she is so unique. She spent about two weeks and worked hard to prepare this very best *habesha* meal to please my friends and me.

For months, I had been preparing to permanently leave the country I love and the land of my origin. I am leaving the place where I was educated, where I established my profession as a journalist, where I met and married my wife, and where all memories of my childhood and young adulthood were created. It is a big change.

I had never thought of coming to Canada until I married my wife Martha Abraham in 2011. She had been my girlfriend since we were teenagers, in high school. Martha and I were born and grew up in the same town, Shashamene, 250 kilometres south of the capital, Addis Ababa. She went to Nairobi as an immigrant and managed to come to Canada. I went to the university and started life in Ethiopia as a journalist. We managed a long-distance love affair for ten arduous years until she came back to Ethiopia for a visit and we were finally able to get married. It was a long and tough journey, but we succeeded through our dedication and determination.

As the month of July 2013 was clocking down, and the short, two-and-a-half months of Ethiopian winter drew to an end, the delightful feast my aunt had prepared for me was in full swing. It was amazingly attended by hundreds of long-time friends, family members, and neighbours. The *Habeshas* adore a feast, congregating in times of happiness or great achievements, public and national holidays, marriage ceremonies, victories and graduations.

Like many others, I fantasized that Canada offered virtually instant prosperity. I was hoping to enjoy a high standard of living as soon as I reached Canada. It was with this understanding in mind that I gave away almost all my belongings to my friends and family. I had no access to sites like Kijiji to sell my things. I had no understanding of the importance of collecting at least some money. I gave away my television and satellite receiver. I gave away my bed and my couch, my other household furniture and my books. In return, they gifted me with traditional Ethiopian clothes, artifacts, spices, and other things they believed would remind me of my country, my loved ones, and the place where I had spent my entire life. One of my best friends, Helen, gave me two *gabbies*, 100 percent Ethiopian hand-made, hand-spun thick cotton fabric blankets. Considering how cold the new place I was heading to, Alberta, actually is, these are among the best gifts I received. I am still using them to fight Edmonton's crazy winter.

As much as I treasured those presents, they incurred me extra expense. I had to buy three extra suitcases and pay airline charges of $150 for each bag to hold the extra food and clothes. Spices, which are common in Ethiopian households and which everyone in the country is proud of, consumed a good deal of space in my luggage.

Warm memories of friendship and kinship are so poignant that they will hopefully stay with me for the rest of my life. But the warmth of that particular enjoyment is not only connected with this celebration, but also because it took place during the transition in my country from the dark, rainy, relatively cold and gloomy season to the warm, bright and blossomy summer and the subsequent hottest and favorable two remaining seasons—fall and spring. In addition to the transition in seasons, the celebration coincided with the shift to a new year.

The Ethiopian New Year is regarded as a time for planning, joy, and the start of a new life. Possessing its own peculiar calendar (13 months with 12 months each having 30 days and the 13th month with 5 days and 6 in each leap year), the Ethiopian New Year falls on the 11 September, except for the leap year when it falls on 12 September. It is one of the happiest times that all people eagerly await to celebrate with new spirit, hoping to have a healthy, joyous, peaceful and prosperous year. They recall memories, visualize what they have passed through over the year, and plan with more stamina and courage for the upcoming year, or as one of the popular national mottos has it—a fresh start to the thirteenth month of sunshine.

Of all the New Years I had celebrated, that New Year came with a lot of surprises and hope. I believed, like many of my friends and fellow citizens, that Canada offered a shortcut to prosperity. Canada, for us in Ethiopia, is considered a land of dollars, luxury cars, oceans of electronic devices, sources of latest fashions, and environments and systems of comfortable life standards.

Most Ethiopians know more about these shiny features or opportunities than the real daily challenges that one could face while living in Canada. So, proud we might be, we still have a bold and hasty generalization about Canada. No one, including myself, sensed the concrete routine confrontations one could face in achieving ultimate goals including the material needs that most of my countrymen and myself are very much obsessed with. Perhaps this perception, which my experience here has shown me was rather naive, exists because of the inappropriate explanations of fellow veteran immigrants.

The media has portrayed the west as heaven on earth. And former immigrants, when they occasionally visit, depict their life in the west as always bright and shiny. These reports led us to believe in a fancy lifestyle with no hardships at all. These portrayals created an undefined obsession, especially in the youth, who are always desperate to escape their country. Definitely this number is increasing year in and year out. Coming to North America is considered a blessing for most Ethiopians.

Nobody really wants to know or understand the challenges new immigrants face in North America. Because of the excessive challenges witnessed in the Middle East and Europe, most Ethiopians and other Africans in general prefer to immigrate to North America. Typically, they entertain a more "happy ever after" narrative and give a deaf ear to what it takes to survive in this part of the world.

However, I was not desperate to come to North America, I simply wanted a reunion with my wife. I don't exactly remember where I read this saying, but it absolutely resonates with my experience here: "A walk of life wears shoes of unknowing hope." That was exactly what my friends and I were feeling at the party in my aunt's house before my departure.

The last late-night meal of, *enjera* with *shiro*—a flat Ethiopian bread served with a spicy stew of chickpeas or broad beans, right after my check-in at the airport—with my best friends Solomon, Helen, and Binyam and my dearest sister Woinishet was extraordinarily great.

Joyful as I was, I always remember that juncture to be a moment of detachment from the community I cherished and the history I am proud of. That moment was in fact synonymous with a fish leaving water. Those friends and family members congregated to express their friendship, love, and respect for me. Excited as they were, their mission to be part of that historic celebration was also dual. It was both a sign of expressing their delight and the moment to get my promise that I would do something for them as I began my journey towards wealth and prosperity.

First things first. When I got to Canada, I focused on survival. I had to purchase new clothes and shoes for the climate and for work. I had to get my driver's license. I had to focus on short- and long-term retraining to fit into the highly competitive environment. The great

Roman playwright Plautus once said: "Unexpected things happen in life more often than you expect." That was exactly the state I was in and I am still in. I never thought of the challenging moments I daily encounter, like consistently paying my bills, generating money for my household needs, purchasing and running a vehicle, and finding money for rent. My struggle is to establish all this before starting to consider the promises I made to my friends and family members before I left. I never thought that the income I generate every other week would barely cover my family's basic needs. I have always been preoccupied with pursuing my education and possessing a house. However, the income I started to generate couldn't stretch to cover the expenses of higher education. The only way I could manage this, I later discovered, was by acquiring a subsidy or student loan from the government. Thanks to the generosity of the Canadian government I am now pursuing my goal of higher education.

My promises, made to my friends and family members, were totally broken. This whole experience has caused me to meditate on Oscar Wilde's famous quote: "To expect the unexpected shows a thoroughly modern intellect." Was I not modern because of my ignorance? Was I wrongly informed? Am I selfish because life in Canada has trapped me into relinquishing my promises once and for all? In my new life, I feel like a soldier. There are no short cuts. Four years after I left my birth country, I am not sure if I can ever fulfill those promises. Right now, I can only promise that I will try to stand on my two feet. It will be some time before I am able to buy the Nikes or Adidas shoes Menge jokingly asked me to get for him at my departure party.

Right now, I can only promise myself to make my most sincere effort to fit into the system and make my life a success. I am convinced that, from now on, I will never promise anyone anything, as life's journey is always unpredictable. I wish my fellow Ethiopians could know and truly sense this transition and forgive me.

2. When Weather Talks Loud

It is not that easy to be an immigrant in Canada, especially when you are over thirty, possessing a completely different cultural, social, and educational background and different experiences. My four-year stay in Canada has been like jumping into a deep gorge from a very high hill. It has been a move from a communal, highly integrated, traditional, and sharing society to a very individualistic, fast-moving, highly law-abiding, and, at times, ignorant society in the sense that so many Canadians I have encountered so far have been quite unaware and even uninterested in my country or my experiences as an immigrant. I found it very tough to adjust to this. This experience brought about anxiety, depression, and hopelessness in the early moments of my settlement in Edmonton.

When I first arrived, I was faced with the challenges of finding work and quickly adjusting to a new culture and way of life. Welcoming as they were, my fellow Ethiopians were themselves preoccupied with the very same challenges and had little time left for companionship and fun. In those early days of adjustment, Mother Nature was therefore my best way out of the scourge of loneliness. It was easy to find solace in nature. In August 2013, Edmonton welcomed me with its blossoming trees, green fields, perfect wind, shiny blue skies, and warm temperatures. Edmonton didn't appear like a city to me, but rather like a park. It wasn't the skyscrapers that grabbed my attention most. It wasn't the vehicles, which fascinated me much. I was drawn to the nature here, which welcomed me with all its heart. Everything was colorful then. Everything was lovely. Everything was perfect.

However, my pleasant welcome didn't last. In two short months, things turned upside down. Edmonton's nature, which had welcomed me with all its gentle summer heart, turned bitter. As September slid into October, I saw the city's young and beautiful body changing into something like a cancer patient passing through cycles of chemotherapy. Edmonton's wind doesn't just blow warm or cold. In the winter, at times, it slaps your face, erodes your ears, smashes your head, cripples your feet, clots or boils your blood, shivers or shocks your veins, and chisels your bones.

One challenge I had as a newcomer to Edmonton that added to my struggle with the weather was finding a job. However, with the help of fellow Ethiopians—Ephrem, Getachew, Samson, and some other members of my community—I got a cleaning job about ten kilometers away from where I live. I didn't have a driver's license since I hadn't learned how to drive in Ethiopia. I had to take a bus which took one and a half to two hours to arrive at my workplace in Strathcona County. Luckily, however, my fellow countryman and fellow coworker, Ephrem, would offer me a ride to my new job. It wasn't easy. I had to wake up at 5 a.m. to catch two buses to Canada Place in order to meet with Ephrem by seven a.m., when he dropped his wife off at work there. Our daily half-hour drives to Sherwood Park were interesting. We discussed our country's history, the ups and downs of life, and exchanged some funny stories. I truly valued Ephrem's open and friendly nature, the way he easily shared his experiences and the way he offered advice about important things I should bear in mind as I adjusted to a Canadian way of life.

I recall being shocked when Ephrem cautioned me against dressing fully in black and covering my face, saying that with the paranoia about terrorism and the colour of my skin, I could be regarded with suspicion. But, of course, it was a matter of survival that as a new immigrant I had to cover myself so fully. The weather required this.

As September passed into October, the wind gave an early warning of the advancing winter. My days as a cleaner in those moments were not fun. In addition to the in-house cleaning service I provided, I also had to caretake the grounds. One of the tasks I dreaded was raking leaves. It was sometimes fun talking to the leaves but not easy satisfying the expectations of my bosses. I enjoyed the falling leaves, the mortals, the helpless beings, as that incredible wind roared with all its regiments. One of my unforgettable memories was when I stopped raking leaves and wrote a short poem.

Leaf or Wind

Mid-morning on a chilly October
as the wind in all directions makes haste and madly roars,
I left my warm room to rake fallen leaves,
gray, separated lungs of trees once and for all gone.
I tried to corral them with my finest rake and rugged arms
but they rebelled, and with the wind, I was at war.
Flying on the air, up and down, here and there,
playing with shivering me, the wind challenged me to a game—
whipping my raked leaves up to dance away,
mocking me, leaving me puzzled
about my own fate, my life, my hopes and dreams.
A young, hopeful African gentleman,
trapped, out of context, out of control.

One Saturday, I saw something I had never seen in my life before. What I witnessed as I left my home for work early in the morning was very hard to comprehend. Snow fell, covering the field up to my knees. Snow carpeted the entire city. It was actually my second surprise. One week earlier, for the first time ever, I had observed snow falling like threads of cotton. I felt like a fool when I spent over an hour staring at the snow pouring gently and softly on the ground. This first experience with snow matched my expectations from my readings and movies. I wished then I was a kid. The snowfall reminded me of my childhood in Ethiopia, when we used to play and spray water at each other as the rain poured. I imagined how the snow would have delighted my friends and I, falling like soft cotton—gentle, very slow, delightful as ice cream. I couldn't stop thinking about the comparison between my childhood in Ethiopia and my present reality in Canada. For a grown-up like me, with only a couple of years left to hit forty, I might be considered insane if I were to be seen playing with snow. One needs to be free, with few concerns in order to fully engage in a playful way with such a phenomenon.

That Saturday morning's experience changed all those simple perceptions I had about Canada. That mid-November morning incident radically changed my easy and fuzzy expectations about this nation. The experience made me confront the way I had not simply and smoothly accepted reality as it was. The new journey I now commenced at the age of almost forty was like bending a firm and matured tree trunk. As the idiom "when the going gets tough, the tough get going" suggests, I kept on asking myself and at times started to murmur: why did I leave my country, terminate my well-established job, escape from the profession I love and all other personal matters?

I tried to act like a scientist. I tried to question my life and my beliefs like a philosopher. However, being rational and calm seemed beyond my capacity. My questions were threaded into the complex experience of my struggle with life and survival in Canada as a new immigrant. The concept of adjustment and the question of survival were at the heart of my limitless contemplations. As a newly wedded man and aspiring to have children, I was trying to reach an understanding of my new life, a fresh start and adjustment. I told myself that people here are living a happy life, even with all the challenges of this fierce weather. I asked myself if I would be able to survive slipping on ice, smashing on the slippery roads and shivering in the cold weather. I told myself that starting a new life has its own ups and downs, its own challenges and threats, its own tough rides.

My good friend Ephrem didn't work on Saturdays. I, on the other hand, needed the money. As I tried to walk to the bus station, I had to trudge through this strange white carpet that stretched to every corner of the city. My shoes which, thanks to my dear wife, Martha, who bought them to make me ready for the real battles on the ground like a fit soldier, were covered with snow. My clothes from top to bottom were covered in snow. I had to walk in slow motion to avoid falling on the slippery ground. As I reached the station and waited for my bus, I felt the deep chill of double-digit below-zero cold. To make matters worse, Saturday is not a good day for those who use the bus in Edmonton. The buses are not as frequent as they are on weekdays. That Saturday for me was therefore a real mess. Despite the confusion I had with my first experience of such weather, the bus which was supposed to arrive at around 7:15 was delayed by almost seven minutes and that created a domino effect on my second bus which was supposed to get me to work on time. I waited for about ten minutes in that chilly weather, but standing in the arctic cold for one more minute was beyond my capacity. I called an information line to know when the next bus would arrive. To my surprise, I was told that I had to wait for an hour. Though it was not the duty and responsibility of the person on the line, I told her that I was new to the city and asked what I should do next, certain I would freeze to death if I waited here another hour. I was told I should spend the next hour in warm comfort. I went to the nearby Edmonton City Centre mall, had tea, warmed myself and stayed there until the time for my bus.

The city had thrown me into complete discouragement and despair. Yes, if there was one thing that made me very much surprised about Edmonton it was that weather. I couldn't stop thinking about it. I couldn't stop asking about it. I couldn't stop contemplating it. I couldn't stop hating it, getting depressed by it, talking about it, and reading about it. Finally, in about fifty minutes, the bus arrived. Life started all over again and the process continued afresh. Forgetting my recent ordeal, I found myself enjoying the snow from inside the bus, feeling warmer.

Sometimes, it is good to be a spectator rather than an actor in life.

Author's Note

I never thought of writing a story about myself. Like many others, I always assumed that people need to have a well-established and successful career, be born into a royal family, achieve celebrity or have done something extraordinary and unique to even begin to consider writing a memoir. But, at some point, I convinced myself that sharing personal surprises, shocks, and wonder could be worth reading for North American readers. Despite the great opportunities out there for new immigrants, my adjustment as a new Canadian has demanded a thick and strong skin and a strong soul to cope with a society well progressed and with a system highly sophisticated and new to me. I saw the challenges in my early moments of immigration and still face the scourge of homesickness, loneliness, and confusion. This drove me to at least tell to my Canadian audience what it meant to be an immigrant from the third world, what an established professional from Africa could face, and what should be done to help new immigrants blend smoothly into the existing community and system. This memoir, therefore, depicts my four-year experience in Canada.

About the Authors

MOHAMED ABDI is a Somali Canadian writer, documentary film-maker, and essayist in advocacy journalism, with a bachelor's degree in Communication Studies. He self-published a nonfiction book, *The Agony of Somalia's Civil War*, in 2004, and an eBook of short stories titled *Mother Somalia: Stories of Hope*, in 2012. He has contributed many articles written in English to both online websites and print newspapers, though English is his second language. Mohamed enjoys reading both fiction and nonfiction in order to understand differing perspectives and to gain inspiration. He likes workouts and short walks to stay energetic, and is married with children.

AKSAM ALYOUSEF was born and raised in Syria. Since graduating from the Higher Institute of Dramatic Arts in Syria in 1994, his primary passion is writing for theatre. In 2001, he travelled to Qatar to work as a theatre instructor and in 2005 he began working as a script writer for children's programs and serials for Al-Jazeera Children's Channel. While in television, Aksam continued to write plays and began writing a feature film. Upon arriving in Canada on January 27, 2016, he began a new play. Aksam participates in many cultural activities in Edmonton and takes English classes through MacEwan University.

Born in Vina del Mar, Chile, on November 15, 1970, SUSANA CHALUT spent her childhood and youth in the city. She studied three years of English Literature and Education at the Catholic University of Valparaiso. She has written short stories and poems since third grade elementary school and has participated in different events and poetry readings in both Vina del Mar and Valparaiso. She arrived in Canada on December 24, 1999, taking ESL and English grammar classes at the University of Alberta. Her book of poetry, *Lights and Shades*, was published by the provincial government in Valparaiso (Cultural Department, 1999). She also placed third in the Andes City poetry contest, 1999. Since coming to Canada she has married, raised two children, and collected many ideas for future poems.

LEILEI CHEN is an academic, a writer, and a translator. She is the author of *Re-Orienting China: Travel Writing and Cross-cultural Understanding*, which was nominated for the Robert Kroetsch City of Edmonton Book Prize and the Wilfrid Eggelston Award for Nonfiction in 2017. She translated Steven Grosby's *Nationalism: A Very Short Introduction* and published its Chinese version with Yilin Press in China in 2017. She teaches English literature, Writing Studies, and Chinese-English translation at the University of Alberta, and is working on the Chinese version of *Re-Orienting China* to be published by East China Normal University Press in Shanghai in 2019.

LUCIANA ERREGUE-SACCHI is a Canadian Argentinian bilingual poet. She holds an MA in Art History from the University of Alberta (2016). Luciana's areas of interest include the politics of canon formation, official portraiture of the Americas, the politics of museum display, and performances of spectatorship. Prior to her graduate work, Luciana studied Law in her native Argentina and was a bilingual art educator at the Art Gallery of Alberta in the years 2004-2005 and 2010-2012. Her poetry has been published online and in print, and addresses the connection between art and memory.

SHIMELIS GEBREMICHAEL moved to Canada about four years ago. Shimelis is originally from Ethiopia where he practiced journalism in both print and electronic mediums. He received his MA in Journalism and Communications and BA in Foreign Language and Literature (majoring in English) from Addis Ababa University, Ethiopia, and holds an MA in Communications and Technology (MACT) from the University of Alberta. He is passionate about making a difference in the community through his literary works (poems, prose, and other forms). He also aspires to continue his journalism career in both English and Amharic. Shimelis is married and blessed with two beautiful children.

In addition to maintaining her own blog, TAZEEN HASAN regularly contributes hard news, investigative pieces, and editorials on topics ranging from science and technology to geopolitics and entertainment for a variety of online and print news outlets. For several years, she contributed travel and history pieces to Asharq-al-Awsat group of newspapers in the Middle East, and Jang and Nawa-e-Waqt groups in Pakistan. She has traveled extensively in the Middle East, Western Europe, parts of South Asia, Africa, and North America with a focus on exploring history and culture. She is fluent in both written and spoken English and Urdu, with a working knowledge of Arabic, Punjabi, and Hindi. She is a graduate of Journalism at Harvard University Extension School.

Born in Toluca, Mexico, ALMA MANCILLA has a degree in Social Anthropology, and holds a PhD in political science from Laval University. Winner of the Benemérito de las Américas Literary Award (Student Category, 2001), the Gilberto Owen National Literary Award (2011), the Ignacio Manuel Altamirano International Narrative Award (2015), and the Jose Ruben Romero Novel Award (2018), she has published three books of short stories, *Los días del verano más largo* (UABJO, 2001), *Casa encantada* (Instituto Mexiquense de Cultura, 2011), and *Las babas del caracol y otros relatos* (Instituto Mexiquense de Cultura, 2014), as well as two novels, *Hogueras* (Editorial Terracota, 2014), and *Archipiélagos* (UAEM, 2015). Her third and fourth novels (*El predicador*, and *De las sombras*) are both to be released in Mexico in 2018.

ANAMOL MANI is a Nepali-born, Canada-based author and journalist. For over one and a half decades he has worked in a wide variety of literary writing and journalism in the Nepali language. He is the author of five books, including the first audio book of a short story in Nepal. In 2009, his first collection of short stories, *Neelima Ra Gaada Andhyaro* (*Neelima and Pitch Darkness*) was published. Three Master's theses and two research papers on gender perspective have been written on that collection at Tribhuwan University. His story "Test-tube Baby Ra Meri Premika" ("Test-tube Baby and My Lover") is popular in Nepal. Other publications include *Sabut* (*Evidence*, 2011), *Aajaka Nepali Katha* (*Contemporary Nepalese Stories*, 2011) and "Nadi Kinar Ma Ubhiyar" ("Standing Beside the River," 2004).

(JA)NINE MUSTER was the child who hid behind a book while the other kids were playing during lunch break at school. Although she has not yet become the next famous author, the Leipziger Volkszeitung (LVZ), a daily print newspaper in Germany, was quite happy with her regular contributions, inspiring locals, on concerts and theatre productions, reportages, and travelogues. Once she finally discovered the internet, she produced online content for Eisbär Media GmbH, a web developer in Leipzig. Being passionate about humans' production of and interaction with their spaces, Nine (pronounced like Nina) moved to Edmonton and recently completed her MA in Sociology at the University of Alberta. Nine cares about language, gets excited when sentences flow smoothly into one another, and is passionate about the Oxford comma. Her biggest dream is to become an author Henry Miller would want to read.

MILA BONGCO-PHILIPZIG is from the Philippines and came to Edmonton on a scholarship for graduate studies on Comparative Literature. After completing her MA at the University of Alberta, she moved to Germany on a scholarship towards a PhD in Cultural Studies. In Munich, she met her husband and they have one son. Mila is the author of *Reading Comics: Language, Culture, and the Concept of Superhero in Comic Books* (2000). In 2016, she published two bilingual children's books, *Sandy Beaches to Snow* and *Goodnight Philippines, Goodnight World*—both reflecting her interests in family, travel, multiculturalism, and diversity.

Born in Hamburg, Germany, KATE RITTNER-WERKMAN immigrated to Canada as a young child and lived in Toronto, Calgary, and Vancouver before finally settling on the prairies in Edmonton. She picked up English along the way. As a child, she was full of stories in both languages and is still fluent in German. Today, Kate has a background in journalism and arts administration. She has written for a variety of newspapers and cultural organizations. Kate is working on her first book, based on searching and finding her biological father in Germany. The essence and point of departure for this work is the hundreds of photographs and three hours of silent film that her father produced during his service as a young front-line soldier in the German Army during the Second World War. A long-kept secret, these materials came under Kate's guardianship when he passed away.

ASMA SAYED is a writer, translator, and academic originally from India. She has published essays, fiction, creative nonfiction, and translations in various anthologies. She writes regularly about issues of social justice in film and media. Her essays have been published in India, Kenya, Canada, and the United States. Asma holds a PhD in Comparative Literature from the University of Alberta, and is a professor of English at Kwantlen Polytechnic University. Her scholarly articles have been published in many journals and anthologies. Her recent editorial works include *The Transnational Imaginaries of M. G. Vassanji: Diaspora, Literature, and Culture* (2018; co-edited with Karim Murji), *Screening Motherhood in Contemporary World Cinema* (2016), *M. G. Vassanji: Essays on His Work* (2014), and *Writing Diaspora: Transnational Memories, Identities and Cultures* (2014). Her co-edited collection of short fiction, *World on a Maple Leaf: A Treasury of Canadian Multicultural Folktales*, was published in 2011.

NERMEEN YOUSSEF is a multilingual Egyptian-Canadian writer and scientist. She holds a PhD in Pharmacology from the University of Alberta and takes immense pride in contributing to developing health policy in the province. She is grateful to her strikingly contrasting home cities— Cairo and Edmonton, for giving her the eyes and ears of an expatriate and to science for teaching her about the freedom of boundless imagination.

About the editor

JULIE C ROBINSON was a Program Coordinator at the Writers' Guild of Alberta (WGA), where she facilitated the Borderlines Writers Circle program. She teaches creative writing at MacEwen School of Continuing Education, and English as a Second Language at Cultural Connections Institute—The Learning Exchange. Her poetry and essays have appeared in Canadian literary journals and online. Her book of poetry, *Jail Fire* (BuschekBooks, 2013) is about the life and work of the nineteenth-century British prison reformer Elizabeth Fry.

Acknowledgements

We acknowledge that the land upon which the Borderlines Writers Circle program takes place is Treaty 6 territory and the traditional meeting ground and home of many Indigenous Peoples, including Cree, Saulteaux, Niisitapi, Métis, and Nakota Sioux. We are grateful for the continued hospitality shown to newcomers.

We are expressly grateful to the Edmonton Arts Council for ongoing financial support of the program, and to Mawenzi House Publishers, particularly Nurjehan Aziz, for assisting us in the effort to make the works of diverse Canadian writers known and available to Canadian audiences. This anthology would not exist without the support of these organizations.

Gratitude must be expressed to Carol Holmes, Executive Director of the Writers' Guild of Alberta (WGA), and Fawnda Mithrush, Executive Director of Litfest: Canada's Original Nonfiction Festival for believing in the program and joyfully promoting participants' work. Special thanks to Ellen Kartz, WGA Communications & Partnerships Coordinator, for the above, for being a sounding board throughout the compilation of this anthology, and for editing expertise. We are also grateful for other organizations that have extended their support: Alberta Association for Multicultural Education, Edmonton Community Foundation, Community Service Learning program at the University of Alberta, and the Edmonton Chinese Writing Club.

Last but not least, the following is an alphabetical list of mentors, supporters and allies whom we love and thank profoundly: Kimmy Beach, Ted Bishop, Myrl Coulter, Ruth Dyck Fehderau, Jannie Edwards, Kathy Fisher, Fahim Hassan, Katherine Koller, Myrna Kostash, Alice Major, Conni Massing, Yukari Meldrum, Peter Midgley, Tololwa Mollel, Omar Mouallem, Jasmina Odor, Pierrette Requier, Shirley Serviss, Anna Marie Sewell, Jaspreet Singh, and SG Wong. There are many more not mentioned here, including family members, friends, and fellow writers who have been with us throughout our writing careers. Thank you.